NIGHT AT KEY WEST

A SIMON WOLFE MYSTERY, BOOK ONE

CRAIG A. HART

I moved through the subtropical night like a jackal on the prowl, only my mission was less that of predator and more the observer. A mercenary observer, but an observer nonetheless. Trailing unfaithful spouses through the Key West streets in the middle of the night didn't top my list of favored assignments, especially for the low wage I'd been offered, but the client was an acquaintance from years back and I'd felt obligated. Besides, while the money hadn't been tops, it was still money. I wasn't proud of my willingness to betray my principles, but those same principles didn't matter a damn to a creditor waiting for a past due payment on a cheap suit or secondhand typewriter.

I shoved my hand into the deep pocket of that cheap suit and felt the one thing I owned outright—a nickel-plated snub-nosed .38 with a wood handle. And even that I hadn't paid cash for but won in a card game when the flop went my way after a string of bad hands. I walked out of that game just after winning the pistol and just before it was raided by the cops. A close shave too, considering the ink on my investigator's license wasn't yet dry. Private investigation wasn't my first love, or even my second, if you want to know the truth of it, but the hours were flexible, and it got me out of the hotel room. And it was a slightly more reliable income stream than the current state of my preferred profession as a writer of fiction. I'd been trying to break into that racket for a while now, and it was no joke.

I watched the woman as she walked, her heels clicking on the sidewalk. I could tell she was going someplace that would make her husband unhappy. A woman dressed like that in a place like this. She turned the corner onto Olivia Street near the house where the writer Ernest Hemingway lived, and I followed, keeping close to the side of the street where the shadows were the deepest. Then, to my surprise, the woman continued onto the property around the back of the house and disappeared through an opening in the fence. I hesitated. Trespassing was one thing. Trespassing onto Hemingway property was quite another. Besides my awe of him as a writer, his reputation made doing something like entering his residence uninvited seem highly unwise. Then again, I needed the skimpy paycheck.

I moved forward to follow the woman and had just passed through the fence when I heard a sound like ice clinking in a glass. A moment later, a light nearly blinded me, and a strong voice said,

"You better have a damn good reason for being here."

I put my hand up to my eyes, trying to block the light. I could see nothing of the man before me, just the stabbing beam of the flashlight. "Would you mind pointing that light somewhere else?"

"State your business and I might. Here to steal? Trophy hunter?"

"I was following the woman who just came this way."

"Can't think of many good reasons a man would follow a woman on a night like this."

"It's not like that."

"Then how is it?"

"I'm on a job."

"Private dick?"

I nodded and then, unsure if the man had seen my gesture, I said, "Yes."

"Jealous husband?"

"That's right."

"Just doing your job," the man said. He lowered the flashlight from my eyes, although a yellow blob still floated before my vision. "Still, not smart. Or legal. Could have been shot, you know."

"Thanks for not doing that."

"It's okay. I'm only armed with this." He held something out that, after squinting with my ruined eyes, I saw to be a beverage. That explained the clinking. It had been ice after all. "What's your name?"

"Wolfe. Simon Wolfe."

"Well, Wolfe," the man said. "I'm Hemingway." He stuck the flashlight in his belt and held out his hand, which I shook after only a momentary hesitation caused by something akin to hero worship.

Feeling as if I should say something, but not sure what,

I opened my mouth and tried to force something out. I was saved from certain humiliation when Hemingway said,

"Has reason for jealousy, you know."

"Who? The husband?"

Hemingway nodded and took a sip from his glass. "She's playing him. But you'll have to let this one go, as the man's a guest of mine. Can't have any friend of mine taken for screwing while on own property."

It was then I first noticed one of Hemingway's idiosyncratic manners of speech—that of occasionally dropping personal pronouns. That night, I chalked it up to the drink in his hand, but I was to discover that these minor omissions were typical, and that, for a man who talked as much as Hemingway, he someway managed to simultaneously exhibit an economy of words.

Hemingway stood there for a moment, observing me and tilting the drink back and forth in his hand. Then he gave a curt nod. "Come on in for a drink."

"I thought you said I'd have to let this one go."

"You do. But I don't fault a man for doing his job."

He turned and walked through the fence opening and onto the property, obviously expecting me to follow. And, of course, I did.

We passed a smaller, two-story structure and headed toward the main house. We entered the house into a kitchen. I'd seen no sign of the woman or her intended rendezvous partner, so I assumed they were either in another room, hiding on the grounds, or had taken refuge in the secondary building. Hemingway went to the freezer and pulled out a chilled glass. He handed it to me.

"Little invention of mine," he said. "Try it out."

I took the glass and looked inside. Water had frozen around what appeared to be whiskey. I put the glass to my lips and felt instantly refreshed as the frigid liquor trickled through the block of ice and ran across my tongue. I felt a smile break across my face. Hemingway saw the smile and returned it.

"If you think that's good, you should go to Havana. There's a drink named for me. A Hemingway daiquiri, called a Papa Doble. They serve it at La Florida in Havana. You should go there."

"I'm not sure I would like it."

"If you like Key West, you would like Havana. How do you find detective work?"

"It's something I do."

"But not because you love it."

"No."

"Didn't realize private dicking paid so well."

"It doesn't. But it keeps me out of an office and off a factory floor."

Hemingway gave another of his curt nods. "That I understand. Plans for the future?"

I looked down into my drink, embarrassed, and when I looked up, I saw that his eyes had sharpened.

"No need for that," he said. "I know what it's like to have big dreams."

"It's not that—I just…"

"You want to write?"

I felt the heat rise into my ears. I nodded. "How'd you know?"

"Two kinds of writers. Those who can't wait to talk about themselves and those who'd rather eat horse shit."

"I guess I'm the latter."

"Those are the ones who write the most," Hemingway said. "Many self-proclaimed writers talk so much about writing that they never do any. They empty the well before they ever put a word on paper. You writing now?"

"I'm trying to work on a book."

"Trying? Or doing?"

"I'm about a hundred pages in."

"When's the last time you wrote?"

"This morning."

He nodded. "That's doing. I work best in the mornings. Get up early, maybe five or six, work until one."

I gathered my courage and asked, "Are you working on anything new?"

"Just published one," he said.

"*To Have and Have Not*," I said. "An incredible book."

"Scribner's liked it. Your stuff published yet?"

"No," I said, feeling the burning in my ears intensify.

"Will get there. I remember before being published. Owe a lot to Scott for that one."

"Scott?"

"Fitzgerald. Pulled a lot of weight at Scribner's, so they had to listen to him. Gave me a plug and they signed me up. What's your racket?"

"Nothing like your work, I'm afraid. I mostly write crime fiction."

Hemingway's expression didn't shift an iota. "Doesn't matter what a man writes, as long as he writes it as true as he can. And what's truer than the underbelly of crime? Write it straight and write it true, and you'll come out fine." He finished his drink and set the goblet on the table. "I wrote some crime."

"You?"

"Sure. Read 'The Killers'?"

I nodded. "I did. It was a great story."

"Nick Adams has a run-in with a couple gangsters."

He saw I had finished my drink and reached for my glass. As I handed it over, he paused in the transfer and then said quickly, "Send over a piece to read."

My mouth went dry. "A piece of my writing?"

"Something not too long but shows what you can do."

"Yes, Mr. Hemingway. Thank you. I'll send something over first thing tomorrow."

"Send it later. I'll be working early, and Pauline will be sleeping late. No damn couriers to disturb either party."

"Of course." I sensed my time had run its course, so I moved toward the kitchen door. "Thanks for the drink. And for not shooting me on sight."

Hemingway chuckled. "Will walk you out."

"It's okay. I can find my way."

"As you'd have it."

He closed the door behind me, but—even though I didn't look back—I was sure he watched me until I left the premises.

2

I wasn't looking forward to meeting my client the next morning and telling him I had no dirt on his dearly beloved. Mike Danby had a reputation as a slugger and more than once had sent a guy to the infirmary in the aftermath of a bar fight. As it happened, Danby didn't appear to be in any shape to cause me serious harm. His eyes were cloudy; his unshaven face was splotchy. He wore a stained undershirt and a wrinkled pair of pants with the cuffs rolled up just past his ankles. He was barefoot and took the news about as well as I imagined he would.

"How long you been following her?" he demanded.

"Two weeks."

"Two weeks! Two goddamn weeks and still you got nothing on her?"

"Nothing solid. No proof. That's what you wanted, isn't it? Proof?"

"Yeah, but I didn't think it'd take this long."

"It's only been two weeks."

"You told me you were a private eye."

Never said I was a good one, I thought. Aloud, I said, "Just give me time. I'll get something."

"What'd she do last night?"

"I lost her."

"You lost her?" His face twisted into a mask of annoyed mockery. "Your tail got shook by a dame?"

"She's smart. You ought to figure yourself lucky."

"I do, wise guy. That's why I'm sore about her stepping out on me. If she weren't a prize, would I care so much?"

"I suppose not."

"Yeah, you suppose not. I suppose not either—I mean, I suppose not too—I also suppose not. What the hell, Wolfe —just get the proof so I can pin her to the wall. That's what I'm paying you for."

"Sure," I said. "About that—"

His eyes narrowed. "You got a lot of nerve."

"It's the beginning of the week. I need it for expenses."

He growled but dug into his pocket and handed me a sweaty and crumpled five-dollar bill.

I took it gingerly, recoiling inside, but knew my land-lord would take it in just about any condition. "Has she come home yet this morning?"

"She must have. Found a wet towel in the bathroom. I didn't see her, though."

"She came home, showered, got dressed, and left again without waking you up?"

"I got a little tight last night," he said.

"You're kidding me, Mike. You?"

"Hey, watch it. I'm not so hungover I can't lick you

around the block. Just because we were buddies once doesn't make any difference now. That debt is paid and paid good." He looked at me, his gaze as sharp as it had been since I'd walked into his room. "It's paid, isn't it?"

"Yeah," I said. "It's paid. You don't owe me anything."

"Then we're square. It's all just business."

I nodded. "Just business."

"Then you find out what that bitch is up to and you get me proof. That's all I'm asking. You hear me?"

"I hear you, Mike." I stuck the money into my pocket and walked out of the room.

Mike Danby lived on the second floor of a two-story rectangular house with a wooden staircase, complete with small landing, providing the only access to the upper area. I paused on the landing and fished a pack of Raleighs from my shirt pocket. I shook one out and then found a match, which I struck against the landing support. The cigarette lit, and I pulled in a puff. I pushed my hat back with a free hand and wiped the back of the hand across my forehead. It was already hot and muggy, and I felt like a warm, wet blanket was wrapped around my shoulders. I squinted my eyes against the sun's glare and walked down the steps. Up on the landing, there had been a slight breeze, but at street level, the air was still—unusual for the island. Nearer the water, there would certainly be moving air, but I wasn't ready to head there yet.

I turned the corner onto Caroline Street and stopped in at a bodega where I knew they had the best bollos in the Keys. The fried black-eyed pea fritters did nothing to cool me down, but they did settle the grumbling in my stomach.

I'd also grabbed a Pepsi-Cola while in the store and I used the bottle opener screwed to the side of the building to pop off the cap. I moved to the welcome shade of a kapok tree, leaned against the large, buttressed roots, and took a long pull on the cola. I let out a breath, belched, and then looked around to see if anyone had noticed. But the street was quiet. Most everyone else was smart enough to stay inside on a hot mid-morning like today. I took another drink and, as I did, ran my hand along the kapok tree. I knew the tree had practical uses, beyond simply looking unique. The bark had been used as an aphrodisiac and many tribes in the French Upper Volta used kapok wood to carve ceremonial masks.

I finished the cola and reluctantly moved back out into the sun. It was time for a real drink. I made my sweltering way down Caroline Street and then turned right onto Duval toward Sloppy Joe's Bar.

The bar had changed locations earlier that year due to the fact that the owner, Joe Russell, resented the increase in rent from three dollars to four. Instead of coughing up the "extortion money," as he called it, he moved the entire operation to its current location. I'd been there during the move and no one, including the customers, even missed a beat when old Joe announced he was moving the bar to the old Victoria Restaurant. Everyone picked up a chair or a table, along with their beer and whiskey glasses, and marched down the road to the new place, where the festivities picked up without a hitch.

I walked inside and bellied up to the bar. The place wasn't busy yet, but I knew later in the day it would get boisterous with live music and dancing. There were times when the roughhousing got so bad that the floor became slippery with blood and beer. That was when Al "Big" Skinner, the three-hundred-pound jovial black bartender, would get out his bat and crack some skulls. I was happy it wasn't yet outright war in the place, because I had some thinking to do.

"What'll you have?" Skinner asked, his wide smile immediately brightening my day.

"Just a whiskey neat," I said, edging sideways onto a bar stool.

Skinner nodded and turned away to get my drink.

I reached into my pocket, pulled out a sheaf of folded papers, and pressed them open flat on the bar. The typing ink had smudged from being in the moist confines of my pants pocket, but it had survived well enough. This was the story I was considering sending over to Whitehead Street —to the Hemingway house. I say "considering," because I wasn't yet sure I was going to take Hemingway up on his offer. It would be silly not to, of course, and countless young writers would have killed their own sisters to have a chance like the one that had simply dropped into my lap. Twenty-four hours earlier, I'd been one of those desperate ones. But now, with the dream come true, I felt almost paralyzed by fear. Suppose he thought it was shit and told me so—which he probably would, if that was his true opinion. Would I ever recover from such criticism? I knew that, no matter how diplomatically put, a low score from Ernest Hemingway would put just about any struggling writer in an early grave, and that I was no exception.

Skinner put my whiskey in front of me. "Whatcha got?" he said, nodding his big head in the direction of my story.

"Nothing much," I said, meaning exactly that. I had chosen the best of my stories, but now that it lay before me on the bar, I felt that it was nothing more than monkey dung on paper.

"This one of yours?" Skinner, knowing I was a writer, picked up the papers and looked at them. He put them down almost immediately, a spark in his eye. "I'm no expert. You should show it to Mr. Hemingway."

"That's the problem. He's offered to read something of mine. I'm supposed to send it over today."

"Then why you in here drinking?"

"Because he's offered to read something of mine and I'm supposed to send it over today."

Skinner's wide, Louis Armstrong grin flashed at me. "Feelin' a little behind the eight ball?"

"Yeah, I guess so. I don't think I'll send it."

"Chance of a lifetime."

"I think I'd rather miss the chance of a lifetime rather than risk being deemed unworthy by someone like Hemingway."

"No risk, no reward."

"It's no risk for me on this one."

"I don't think that's a choice for you to make," Skinner said. "Not anymore, anyway."

"What do you—?"

A heavy hand fell on my shoulder.

"What's the matter, kid?" a voice said. "You a writer, or aren't you?"

I started visibly. Skinner chuckled and then wandered off to help another customer.

Hemingway eased up to the bar next to me. "Sorry to startle you."

"No, it's just—I wasn't expecting to see you here at this hour."

"Not usually. Leaving soon for Madrid and had a dust-up with Mrs. Hemingway. Needed to get out." He pointed at my story. "That what you were deciding not to send me?"

I nodded.

"Let's see it."

My insides turned to gelatin. The only thing worse than having Ernest Hemingway read my writing was for him to read it right in front of me. But the order was not to be refused, so I slid the pages over to him.

He began reading immediately, and I watched as his eyes moved across and down the pages. I was surprised by the attention he was devoting to the read. After what seemed like hours, but what could not have been more than ten minutes, he finished the story and replaced it on the bar. During the reading, Skinner had placed a whiskey in front of him and he now paused to throw some back.

"You've got it, kid," he said.

I felt like I might throw up. I wasn't sure exactly what he meant by "it," but I assumed it to be good.

"You write simple and true. What's more, you've let out more than you put in."

I shrugged. "It's just a crime story."

"Gotta let that go, kid. Told you before—doesn't matter

what a man writes, as long as he writes it the best he can, as true as he can. This is as true a story as have read in a long time."

"It's a made-up story."

"That's not what I mean. Sometimes the truth can only be told in fiction. To be honest, kid, I took a chance reading this. Expected it to be like those in the mystery magazines. But it's a real story. Main character, Sam—he isn't a safecracker just for the sake of it. He has motive—motive that involves the reader, makes them pull for the guy."

"You mean the part about his dying mother."

"Backstory. That's what most of today's crime writers miss. They think a lot of movement is enough, but there's rarely motivation for it. They confuse movement with action. True action happens for a reason, kid. Never forget that."

I nodded. "I think I know what you mean."

"Not to say there aren't spots for improvement."

Here it comes, I thought.

"Whole first page can go. Serves no purpose."

"I was trying to set up the story."

Hemingway pulled at his whiskey. "Better to just begin story. Learned that from Scott, back when was writing *The Sun Also Rises*. Advised me to cut first few pages. I did, and book was better for it. Scott wrote well early—such a gift—but destroyed by drinking and that crazy, jealous, bitch of a wife." Hemingway finished his whiskey. "Speaking of which, any more leads on your woman?"

"No," I said. "And the client was less than pleased that I lost the opportunity."

Hemingway pushed away from the bar. "You'll get another chance. Until then, come by for drinks tonight. Boxing match at the house, last before I leave for Madrid."

I watched him leave the bar, big shoulders swinging, and him walking on the balls of his feet like a boxer in one of the evening's matches. I turned back and caught sight of Skinner smiling at me. He gave me a quick nod and then turned back to his business.

AROUND NOON, I went around to the First National Bank where Mike's wife worked. She'd be taking her lunch and smoke break then, as I knew from previous reconnaissance, and was hoping to find her chatting up a male friend. As I approached the building with its unique, alternating pattern of red and yellow brick and distinctive cupola, I saw Mrs. Danby, wearing a green dress, exit the front door and turn left onto Front Street. I followed her to Pepe's, where she disappeared inside. I debated going in after her. While we weren't pals or anything, she would certainly recognize me on sight, as I'd been around Mike's since I'd returned to Key West. The frequency of the visits, although never frequent, dropped precipitously not long after, with Mike explaining that Thelma found me to be a bad influence on her husband. I'd found this insulting, since it was always Mike who started any trouble we got into, but I also knew that it was in Mrs. Danby's best interest for her to blame others for the scrapes her husband found himself in.

Making up my mind, I pulled my hat low and went inside. At first, I didn't see her, but then I caught a glimpse of green fabric sticking out from a booth near the back of the room. I couldn't see the rest of her, but after shifting my position as much as I dared, I did see there was a man sitting across from her.

"You can sit wherever you like, sir," said an employee named Juan, a dark Latin man with a thin black moustache.

"Thanks," I said, choosing a spot where I could see Mrs. Danby's booth but that afforded me a measure of safety were she to suddenly look around the room. I kept my hat on and pulled low, aware of how suspicious this made me look, but not caring. The last thing I wanted was for my mark to know I was tailing her. That would make my job infinitely more difficult.

I ordered a drink but passed on food as I sat, waiting. I waited for almost an hour before the green fabric shifted and a leg came into view. She was exiting the booth. The man slid out, stood up, and put money on the table. Then he held out his arm for the woman.

Gutsy, I thought. Key West wasn't a big place, and here they were courting in plain sight.

Then I saw why the boldness wasn't so bold—the woman wasn't Mrs. Danby. The goddamn woman had given me the slip. She must have walked in the front and out the back.

"Juan!" I waved to the man who'd seated me.

He came over. "Yes, Mr. Wolfe?"

"Did you see a woman in a green dress come in about an hour ago and then leave by the back way?"

"That woman?" He pointed at the imposter.

"No, another one. She would've just walked in and out."

"I am sorry, but I saw no one else wearing a green dress. Of course, I have been busy and could easily have missed her."

I swore but knew there was nothing for it. I'd been had and good. What was worse, the move suggested she knew she was being watched or, at least, suspected it strongly enough to take evasive action. I hightailed it back to the bank and saw Mrs. Danby already back at work behind the counter. It could have been my imagination, but I thought she looked rather pleased with herself as she counted out bills and then handed them to her current customer.

3

That evening, a fight was already underway by the time I presented myself at Hemingway's home, this time coming in the front way like a respectable individual. I was met by a woman with short, dark hair and a smile that was welcoming, although I thought I sensed sadness behind the mask. She introduced herself as Hemingway's wife, Pauline. She led me through the house and out the back to the action. Two boxers were going at it in a makeshift ring next to the separate two-story structure I'd noticed on my first nocturnal visit. Hemingway bobbed his way around the ring, acting as cheerleader and referee. We stood watching the proceedings.

"He certainly seems to be enjoying himself, doesn't he?" I said.

Pauline inclined her head. "Ernest is a man who loves action and, if I may say without making him sound something of a brute, a measure of violence as well."

I could understand what she meant. As the blows fell,

Hemingway's eyes almost seemed to glow as his blood coursed hotter, and I felt myself getting into it as well, the lust for battle kindling in that ancient part of a man's soul.

"I'm not a fan of boxing myself," Pauline said. "Ernest leaves for Spain soon and I'm thinking of putting a pool in where the boxing ring is now. He's spoken of wanting a pool, but I'm not sure how he'll take it." She turned to me suddenly. "Don't speak of it to him; I'm planning it as a surprise."

"My lips are sealed," I said, although I wasn't sure if Ernest was a man who would appreciate such a surprise. Then again, his wife would certainly know him better than I did.

"But I'm being a terrible hostess," Pauline said. "Would you like something to drink?" She led me over to a table laden with drinks and food. I selected a bottle of Old Union and then a slice of toasted bread with a slab of turtle meat and horseradish sauce.

Pauline excused herself as more guests arrived, and I was left alone to eat and drink. A sudden squawk behind me caused me to start and I turned to see a peacock standing under a nearby fig tree, observing me closely with its beady, suspicious eyes.

"Don't mind them," said a voice. "Think they're too good for everyone." It was Hemingway, once again managing to come up on me unaware. I hadn't even noticed the fight had ended in a knockout.

"Magnificent birds," I said.

"Gift from Jane Mason," Hemingway said, then added

casually, "May explain why Mrs. H. doesn't much care for them."

I didn't pursue the remark, choosing instead to praise the turtle meat and beer.

Hemingway ignored the compliment. "You ever box?"

I shrugged. "I've done a little. I'm not in a class with these men, though."

"Not many are. Those are professionals. The ring's open now—we should go a couple of rounds."

"You and me?"

"Sure."

The thought of landing a glove on Ernest Hemingway made my blood run a little cold. "No, I don't think—"

"Come on, kid—I'll go easy on you. No head shots, choose your own glove weight, two rounds at the most."

It was clear the invitation did not include an option to decline, and I didn't want to insult him by turning him down. I nodded slowly. "Just a couple of rounds."

He broke into a grin so wide that one might have thought he'd been given a million dollars. I was beginning to see why the man was so revered, beyond his obvious genius. Charisma could have been his middle name. When you were with him, it felt as if you were the only person in his world and, very soon, pleasing him became the only thing on your mind.

Still, I had misgivings as I chose a pair of ten-ounce gloves and fitted my headgear. Hemingway also wore headgear, which surprised me a little.

"Have to protect my capital," he said, pointing at his head. "Without that, I'm out of business but fast."

CRAIG A. HART

We assumed our fighting stances and I immediately saw the change in Hemingway. His face, which just a moment before had been alight with almost childish pleasure at my having agreed to box, had taken on a much more intense expression. His eyes flickered with adrenaline and an eagerness for combat. And I knew then, even if I had been capable of it, that I should not beat him.

The fight began slowly, as we circled each other, looking for openings. Then Hemingway moved in fast and landed a stinging blow to my right side. I spun away, and he let out a bellowing laugh.

"Now you're moving, kid!"

We continued circling, with occasional forays into battle, until Hemingway rushed in full bore, fists flying, lips drawn back, teeth bared. My hesitation to engage was completely overridden by sheer self-preservation and I struck back twice, one blow a solid strike to his shoulder that turned him halfway around. He looked surprised, then by equal parts angry and pleased. He moved in again, this time landing a fist on the left of my headgear.

"No head strikes!" the referee shouted.

Hemingway was beyond hearing. He pressed his advantage, peppering my forearms with punches. At last, I heard a bell signal the end of the round. Hemingway backed away but did not relax, and the second round began almost immediately. Back he came, head low, eyes gleaming out beneath a darkened brow that glistened with sweat.

He's going to take me out, I thought.

From that moment on, it became a matter of sheer survival as Hemingway's big frame jostled me around the ring, his gloved fists creating a staccato sound as they probed my defenses.

Then he was in so close I could smell the alcohol on his breath.

"Come on, fight back, you sonofabitch," he growled.

And I discovered myself in the unenviable position of having to displease my idol. If I fought back too well, I was certain he would take exception. But neither was he planning to let me simply wait the fight out to the end. He expected a challenge, but one that he could eventually master.

I began responding to his jabs with counterattacks, measured but calculated, inflicting just enough damage to appear invested in the fight. In truth, I didn't care at all and would have been happy to simply lie down on the dirt floor of the ring if it meant the fight could be over.

My staged attacks invigorated Hemingway and he seemed confident that I was now fighting to my potential, not knowing I was holding back. Thus comfortable with my low skill level, he allowed his guard to drop and his punches became wider and less coordinated, more concerned with power than finesse.

And then he brought his right forward and I saw it—a beautiful opening straight to the point of that strong jaw, a path to a knockout if I'd ever seen one. The temptation was almost too much to bear. Not only could I be the man who knocked out Ernest Hemingway, but I could heal the shredding that my reputation had taken during my absurd fighting display. But I also realized that the cost of these would be high. I didn't believe Hemingway would be the type to come out of a knockout, smile, and clap me on the back as having proven to be the better man in the ring. I could take my moment of glory, but I'd be giving up so much more. And so, I let it pass. The opening closed and, as it did, the bell rang to end the second round. I let my gloves fall to my sides and had just turned to leave the ring, when something like a hammer crashed into the side of my head and everything went pitch black.

I AWOKE to find a ring of faces above me, the most concerned of which appeared to be Hemingway's.

"You took a good punch, kid," he said, reaching down and grasping my wrist. He hoisted me up. I immediately regretted the decision to stand as the world went into a tailspin and the turtle meat sandwich threatened to revisit the world. "Needs a drink," Hemingway barked out. "Give the kid a drink."

A drink wasn't at all what I wanted, but someone shoved a snifter of brandy under my nose. The smell alone had a somewhat restorative effect, and after I tossed it back, my brain cleared enough to remember what had happened.

"You sucker punched me!" I said, trying to point an accusing finger toward Hemingway but realizing I was still wearing the boxing gloves. I began working at the laces with my teeth, but Hemingway took over the job of untying them.

"Don't get sore, kid," he said. "I threw the punch before

your guard dropped, just as the bell rang. You turned and dropped your guard and it was too late to stop the blow."

I didn't know whether or not to believe him, but there was no point in pressing the issue. I removed my head gear and strained my neck first one way and then another, popping the joints and making sure everything was in good working order.

And then I saw her.

"You're okay, kid," Hemingway was saying. I hardly heard him. I was looking at the woman—Mrs. Danby—who was hanging on the arm of one of the regulars I'd seen at Sloppy Joe's, part of Hemingway's mob of buddies. Hemingway saw my look and followed the gaze. "Thought she'd be here," he said. "Partly why I asked you. To make up for having to turn you away the last time."

"But she's...doesn't everybody know that she's Danby's wife?"

"Course they do. And everybody knows something else too."

"I don't follow."

"Open your eyes, kid," Hemingway said impatiently. "The woman's a bona fide whore. Been sleeping around town long as I've known her. Only ones who don't know this are that louse of a husband and you. Guy with her, he's a hundred deep in her already."

"She's taking money for sex?"

"Know another kind of bona fide whore?"

"I thought you just meant she slept around a lot."

"She does. Only she gets paid to do it."

4

I took Mike Danby out to breakfast the next morning, partly because I felt like shit for what I was about to tell him and partly because I hoped being in a public place would lessen the likelihood of violence.

We went into the Electric Kitchen on Fleming Street and paid our forty-five cents each for Rhoda Baker to put together two of the heartiest-sized breakfasts offered by the inaptly named establishment.

"Electric Kitchen," Mike growled. "The only electric things in this entire joint are those naked bulbs dangling from the ceiling."

I couldn't argue with him. The modern name did little to inspire confidence, once you got a look at the simple wooden structure with the tin roof and wrap-around porch awning. But the food was cheap, good enough, and filling. And it offered a straight shot onto Fleming Street if I needed to flee Mike's wrath when he found out his wife was a common prostitute.

I waited until halfway through the meal of thick Cuban coffee, stale slices of bread, avocados, and smoked fish— after I'd eaten enough to make my money worth it and just as Mike and I had pretty much used up all the conversation we were likely to have.

"Got a lead on your wife," I said, casually sipping at coffee that tasted like burnt sugar.

Mike stopped eating immediately. "Yeah? What's the story?"

"You're not going to like it," I warned.

"Hell, I already know that."

"Yeah…but it's worse than you think."

"How could it be worse?"

"She's a whore, Mike."

Mike threw back his head and laughed loudly, causing everyone in the place to look in our direction. "Goddamn right, she's a whore! Why the hell you think I hired you?"

"Keep it down," I said, my voice the loudest, wettest stage whisper ever heard.

At last, something pierced into Mike Danby's big, stupid head and he realized I was being serious. "What do you mean, she's a whore?"

"She's a whore, Mike. In every sense of the word."

Mike stood up so suddenly that the table flipped onto its side, sending the entire breakfast into my lap. I stood up as well, prepared for anything.

"That's a goddamn lie!" he shouted, his face turning purple.

A few people got up and began edging their way toward the door. I didn't blame them. I wanted to do the same but seeing my hope that a public place would keep a lid on Mike's explosive anger was misplaced at best, I felt a responsibility to keep him from destroying Rhoda's business.

"Keep a lid on it, Mike," I said. "Let's go on outside."

"The hell I will! You're going to take that back or I'll stove your head in."

"It's the truth, Mike. Getting mad at me won't solve anything."

And then he came at me, charging like a bull, his head lowered, meaty shoulders braced. The distance was short and so he didn't have much time to build up a head of steam, but just the same, it was a formidable sight and reminded me of our high school football days. I could see him now, rushing the ball handler in his padded pants and leather helmet—except now I was the target. I dodged to one side at the last moment and Mike went crashing out onto the porch, carrying the entire screen door with him.

Rhoda flew in from the kitchen, a spatula held high and dripping hot grease. She was screaming something incoherent, but I suspected it had something to do with Mike going straight to hell.

I followed Mike out, my hands held out in front of me, trying to reason with him, tell him it wasn't my fault, that I was only doing the job he'd hired me to do. But Mike wasn't having any of it, and as soon as he saw me step onto the porch, he wound up and came at me again, this time with more finesse—if such a word could ever be used to describe anything Mike did—his fists flying and large head bobbing back and forth.

"No one calls my wife a whore," he shouted, coming forward like a boxing gorilla.

I gave up trying to reason with him, because it was clear he was long past that. But neither could I turn tail and run; Key West was too small a place to get away with anything that might be considered cowardice. While I wasn't exactly afraid of Mike, I knew from personal experience that a blow from his ham-sized fist left a lasting impression. There was nothing to be done, however, and so I put up my defenses and decided to die with my boots on.

We were going at it good and proper when a man came running up Fleming Street calling out Mike's name. This was notable, mostly because people didn't run in Key West unless they absolutely had to. Running and overly exerting oneself were not considered virtues in our little island paradise, especially by the Conchs, which was what the locals were called. Not to say they were lazy by any stretch; it was simply that they had certain priorities and none of them required haste. They believed in working smarter, not harder, and took the relaxed reputation of the island quite seriously. They missed being a tropical island by under a hundred miles, and for Key West, that was damn well close enough.

It took a minute for Mike to realize someone was calling his name, but when he did, he seemed to recognize the significance. He half-dropped his fists and glanced once at the man, who by now was buzzing around the two of us like No-see-ums on a still day in a mangrove forest.

"What do you want, Brucie? Can't you see I'm busy?"

"It's important, Mike."

"So's this." Mike took a swing at my face, but I saw it coming and easily sidestepped the effort.

"It's about your wife," Brucie said.

"Yeah, well, so's this." Mike glared at me, but this time kept his fists to himself. Finally, he backed out of my punching range to avoid being suckered and looked full at Brucie. "Okay, what's so all-fired important?"

"Maybe we should go inside," Brucie said. His face was all pale and slick. I'd thought at first it was from running in this heat, but now I could see something in his eyes that told me it was far worse.

"You'll tell me here and now," Mike demanded.

Brucie gathered himself, swallowed hard, and then said, "Your wife, she's…she's—"

"She's what, Brucie? My wife is what?"

But I already knew the answer, and so did Mike. Before Brucie could bring himself to say the words, Mike had sat down hard on the street. Just sat right down on his ass, and so help me God, he started to cry. His big head sort of lolled on his chest and his shoulders heaved. The hands that a minute earlier had been so intent on cracking my skull now opened and closed obsessively, as if softening a lime before slicing it open to squeeze over a drink. I moved in and placed a hand on his shoulder, half expecting him to shrug it away, but he didn't. He just sat there, sobbing like a little kid.

"How'd it happen?" I asked.

"Manager of the Overseas Hotel found her. In the bathtub."

"Drowned?"

"Throat cut. Ear to ear. Manager said he'd never seen so much blood."

Mike let out a wail that could have been heard on Trumbo Point.

"Okay," I said to Brucie, "that's enough. Let's get Mike home."

"The police will probably want to talk to him."

"That's their problem. Let's just get him home."

We each took an arm and managed to get Mike on his feet. We pushed our way through the little crowd that had begun gathering and steered Mike back to his second-floor apartment. By the time we arrived, he'd stopped blubbering and lapsed into repetitive mumbling. It was a chore getting him up the stairs, but at last we got him inside and set him down on the side of the bed. He promptly fell over backward and continued his low muttering.

"Oh god, I can't believe it happened—it finally happened—can't believe she's dead—poor Thelma—never thought this would happen—I can't believe it—oh god, is it true—?"

I moved away from the bed and pulled Brucie along with me until we were back outside on the wooden landing.

"Did you see the body?" I asked.

Brucie nodded. "I was staying across the hall from— that room. I was reading a paper when I heard the manager give a shout for help. I jumped out of bed, threw on a pair of trousers, and went into the hallway to see what was happening. I saw the door of the room across from me standing open and so I poked my head inside.

'Everything okay in there?' I said, and the manager shouted back that something really bad had happened and to call the police."

"And did you?"

"Did I—?"

"Call the police."

"Yes. Well—first I went inside the room to determine the exact state of emergency. And that's when I saw Mrs. Danby in the tub. Completely naked. Her head was leaned back on the edge of the tub and her eyes—those blue eyes —were still open and staring up at the ceiling. Her throat was cut clean across and the wound gaped like a second mouth, because her head was thrown back. Her real mouth was open, like she'd been gasping for air."

"She probably had," I said. "Sounds like you got quite an eyeful."

"More than I wanted. Must've been quite a toothpick to cause a cut like that."

"A what?"

Brucie grinned sheepishly. "Sorry. That's old country slang for a big knife."

"Ah. Is the body still there?"

"Unless they've carted her away."

I lit a fire under my heels and got to the Overseas just in time to see them taking the body from the bath. An officer stepped forward to block my path before seeing it was me.

"Oh," he said. "It's you."

Not the warmest greeting I might have preferred, but it was better than getting tossed out on my ear. He let me step just inside the door, close enough to confirm the description given by Brucie. I turned to the officer, a fellow named Barnes.

"Any idea what happened?"

"Just what it looks like. Dead dame. No idea of the specifics. They're taking her down to Marine Hospital to get checked out. I don't know if they'll find anything, but it could be murder or a suicide."

"A suicide?"

"Could be."

"I've never heard of a woman committing suicide by cutting her own throat. Read about men doing it, but it's rare either way."

Barnes shrugged. "That's out of my wheelhouse. You're welcome to follow the meat wagon down to Marine and talk to Big Louis. Maybe he can tell you more."

"Can I look around the room?"

Barnes pulled me aside as two men exited with the late Mrs. Danby on a gurney and covered in a white sheet. "I guess. Don't touch anything, though, and make it quick. I gotta get over to Mike's."

I stepped closer to the bath and walked completely around it. There was no water in the tub and the bottom and sides were still slick with blood.

"Was there water in the tub when you got here?" I asked.

Barnes shook his head. "Nope. I figured she got in, so she wouldn't make a mess, and took off her clothes, so they wouldn't get ruined."

"Who cares about that stuff when you're planning suicide?"

Barnes shrugged. "That's a woman for you."

I spotted something and stooped to look at it.

Barnes stepped forward. "What is it?"

"The straight razor."

"Oh, yeah. I saw that. Don't touch it."

"I won't touch anything, Barnes, goddammit. Just wanted a closer look."

"I figure she drew it across her throat and then let it fall from her hand over the side of the tub and onto the floor."

"Maybe," I said. "Want company over to Mike's?"

Barnes nodded. "I might need it."

We left the hotel, with Barnes leaving strict instructions with the manager to keep any and all curiosity seekers out of the room, and went toward Mike's via a shaded lane that reminded me of some of the streets in New England when I'd been there for higher education. But there, the resemblance ended. Whereas New England was still somewhat bound by Puritan tradition, Key West went to great lengths to avoid such entrapments. "Live and let live" was the only credo worth anything, at least in the view of Conchs. Polite society was a rare breed in these parts and that was just how Key West liked it. Anyone found sporting a superior attitude could expect hard times on the island and was expected to shape up or ship out.

Outside Mike's wooden, unpainted rooming house, Barnes took the lead.

"Better let me go first," he said. "I'm not expecting trouble, but you know how Mike can be."

I did indeed and had no issue letting the officer precede me up the stairs and onto the landing. He knocked on the door, waited, and then the handle jiggled and rattled from the inside. The door opened a few inches and Brucie's narrow face peered out at us. His eyes, generally frozen in a squint, closed even further when he saw Barnes. He saw me next and relaxed a little, but still held the door mostly closed.

"Let us in, Brucie," Barnes said. "We need to talk to Mike."

I was surprised to hear Barnes say "we" and assumed I was being used as a method of gaining entrance. Brucie picked up on it as well.

"You two workin' together?"

I opened my mouth to play down that idea, but Barnes ploughed ahead.

"He's consulting for us," he said before I could say a thing. "Let us in."

"You ain't takin' him in, are you?" Brucie asked. "He didn't do anything. You can ask Wolfe. They were havin' breakfast together."

A fight is more like it, I thought. But I kept my mouth shut, figuring Mike didn't need any aspersions cast on his character at the moment.

"I'm not taking him in. Not yet. Unless, of course, he won't talk here. Then I won't have much choice but to take him."

Brucie hesitated, then I heard Mike's voice from inside the room.

"Let them in, Brucie. I don't have anything to hide."

The door opened enough to let me and Barnes inside, then closed promptly behind us. Mike was sitting on the bed. He held a glass in one hand and sipped at it as he fixed us—mostly Barnes—with an expression that was an odd combination of disdain, grief, and fear.

Brucie went over to stand near him, a bundle of protective yet largely ineffectual energy, like a Chihuahua watchdog. "You don't got to say nothin', Mike. They got nothin' on you. You don't got to say nothin'."

"It's okay, Brucie," Mike said, the master to his dog. "I don't have anything to hide." He watched as Barnes stepped into the center of the room and placed his thumbs in his belt. I hated him for that stance; it was a power play and that was all.

"I guess you know about Mrs. Danby," Barnes said.

Mike nodded. "I know she's dead. That's about it."

"Then you know she was probably murdered."

Again, Mike nodded. "Doesn't figure someone would cut their own throat."

This was a new one on me. At the hotel, Barnes was all set to mark it off as a suicide, but now that he faced the grieving husband, his story had changed, and he'd adopted an aggressive tone to match his posturing. Clearly an act, and I hated him a little more for that.

"We'll have to see what coroner says about it, but she can't have been there long. Bodies don't last long in this climate and she was fresh as a daisy. Just off the top, I'd say she was killed early this morning. Last night at the very latest."

"I was here all last night," Mike said. "And went to breakfast with Sims."

Barnes turned to me. "That right?"

I nodded. "I met Mike here and we went down to the Electric Kitchen."

"Anyone else there who can verify that?"

"Sure," I said. "Rhoda will back me up. And I'm sure the others there will remember." I didn't elaborate on why the other diners would be sure to remember our breakfast excursion. Barnes could find that out on his own time.

"Still," Barnes said, playing the sleuth all the way to the hilt, "you would've had time to kill your wife and then get back here in time to meet Simon."

"It doesn't matter if I had time or not," Mike said. "I didn't do it."

"Any ideas about who might want your wife dead?"

Mike looked at me and I knew what he was thinking: that depends on how many people she slept with and if any of them owed her money. I knew that was what he was thinking, because I was thinking the same thing. Mike shook his head slowly and looked back at Barnes.

"No," he said. "I can't think of anyone who would want to hurt Thelma. She was a good woman. Never hurt anyone, never had an unkind word to say."

Now he was laying it on too thick. I wanted to send him a signal, something to tell him to back down the throttle. It was natural to want to only remember the good things about the deceased, but the accolades could wait until the funeral. Now was the time to play it down and close to the vest. I searched Barnes' darkly-tanned face for any clue to his state of mind, but he could have played a pretty good hand of poker and I saw no tell.

"Well, you sit tight," Barnes said, taking his thumbs

from belt and hitching up his pants. "I'm sure we'll have more questions once Big Louis gets a look at the body. You're not planning to leave town, are you?"

Mike coughed out a hard laugh. "And go where?"

"Just checking. Stick around. If you decide you need to go somewhere, check with me first." He turned and left the apartment without so much as a by your leave.

As soon as the door had closed, Mike drained his glass and stood up, heading for the cabinet for another drink.

"Don't you worry, Mike," Brucie said, tailing him. "We got your back."

Mike opened the cabinet and pulled out a bottle of gin. He splashed some into the glass and returned to the bed, where he sat down heavily. He looked at me. "Did you see her?"

"Yeah, Mike. I saw her."

"Was it bad?"

"It was pretty bad, Mike."

Mike took a drink. "Goddammit. I can't believe it."

"Do you have any ideas about it? I know you told Barnes you didn't, but I wouldn't blame you for lying to that little leech."

"I don't know anything. Hell, I didn't know the full story until this morning. Until then, I thought she was just messing around on the side."

"You had no idea she was running a game?" I found this a little hard to swallow. I hadn't known either, but I hadn't been married to Thelma Danby. I'd never been married at all but was pretty sure I'd notice if my wife was gone at all hours.

Mike shook his head.

"What about money?"

"Money?"

"Extra money. I don't think she was turning tricks for a lark. Did you notice her having new things you couldn't afford?"

Mike thought about it. "I guess there was some stuff. I asked her once and she said a relative in Arkansas sent her stuff. That seemed okay with me. They'd always been close, and her cousin had married some guy whose family had gotten rich off a cotton ginning business." He drained his drink once more and stood, a little unsteadily, looking like a man who wanted yet another round. Before heading to the cabinet, he looked at me, his eyes like those of a hound dog that's been told it's too old to hunt. "You'll help me, won't you, Sims? You won't hang me out to dry with the likes of Barnes. You wouldn't do that, would you?"

"We're not gonna leave you, Mike," Brucie said, but Mike ignored him and kept looking at me.

I nodded slowly. "I guess I'm still in your employ. If you want me to look into it, I'll do it. As long as you know that I'll follow the trail wherever it leads. I'm no fix-it man. If the trail turns back to you, that's where I'll follow it."

Mike nodded. "That's jake with me," he said, and went back to the cabinet to refill his glass.

5

That afternoon, I stopped in at the courthouse on Simonton Street, in the hope of cornering Franklin Arenberg, better known as "Big Louis." Arenberg was a native Conch who had his fingers in many law enforcement pots in Key West, including those of justice of the peace and coroner ex officio.

When I arrived at the courthouse and went inside, I found Arenberg busily conducting a hearing complete with defendant and defending attorney. I stepped just inside the door and waited for them to complete their business.

The defense attorney, a man I knew only by sight, stepped forward. He was slight of build, with salt and pepper hair cut short at the sides. His hands showed signs of rheumatism onset, but the set of his jaw and his bulldog-like demeanor prevented any assumption that he might not be up to any job to which he set his mind. His grey suit showed sweat stains down the back and armpits. I didn't blame him for this—the afternoon was heavy and ruggedly hot, and the inside of the courthouse felt like a blast furnace, even with all available fans going full tilt.

"Your honor," the defense attorney said, "my client is not guilty by virtue of the following: according to Florida statute—"

Arenberg interrupted by banging the flat of his palm down on the stand. "Don't start feeding me that hogwash, Mr. Harris," he said. "The only statutes I'm acquainted with are those in the local cemetery." He stood up and put on his suit jacket, which had been hanging limply over the back of his chair. "Defendant is hereby held over for trial in criminal court."

Attorney Harris held out his hands in supplication. "But, your honor, if you'll only just listen to—"

"Bailiff!" Arenberg barked. "Clear the courtroom!"

I looked around for a bailiff, but no such individual was in sight, nor did one appear. This minor fact didn't slow down Arenberg at all. He barreled around the desk and down the center of the room, heading right for the door by which I was standing. Deaf to the continuing pleas of the defense attorney, Arenberg banged through the doors and out into the foyer. I followed closely behind but waited to address him until we were out on the street.

"Mr. Arenberg?"

He stopped abruptly and whirled. "Who are you?"

"Wolfe, sir. Simon Wolfe."

He put his finger on his chin and assumed an attitude of deep concentration. "Wolfe…Simon Wolfe…Wolfie boy… yes, that sounds familiar. Well, what the hell do you want?"

"It's about Mrs. Danby."

"Ah, yes."

"I was hoping to get some information about her death."

"Haven't even seen the body myself," Arenberg said. "Been tied up in court all day. I'm headed to Marine Hospital now to perform my coroner's duties. Come along if you like. I seem to recall you're an investigator of some kind."

"Yes. A private operator."

"Then you should find this interesting." Arenberg motioned for me to follow and we went to a black Terraplane parked on the street. I was about to comment on the short distance, but the heat made a strong case for as little physical activity as possible. We got in and Arenberg started the engine. Making a wide turn on the road, we headed down Caroline Street toward Front.

Once at the hospital, Arenberg parked on the street once more. We got out and made our way up to the hospital, with its white awnings and steep concrete front steps. The building had been one of eight Marine hospitals designed by Robert Mills, an architect and engineer who was well-known as a protégé of Thomas Jefferson. Among Mills' other work were several landmarks in Washington, D.C., including the Washington Monument.

We climbed the steps and then Arenberg stopped just outside the doors. He turned to me.

"Now, I know you're a writer," he said, his voice abrupt and mildly accusing. "And you know I'm not a medical man by trade. I don't want you writing up that I don't know what I'm doing or that I do shoddy work."

I was somewhat taken aback but nodded my assent.

"I'm not here for a story," I said. "I'm just looking for information, that's all."

Arenberg seemed satisfied with that, and we entered the hospital. We walked down a bare hallway until we came to a set of swinging doors. Arenberg barged in and I followed close behind. The room was dim and, while not cool by any means, was the most comfortable room I'd been in that day. Comfortable, at least, by temperature standards. The room's setting was more than a little unnerving. In the center was a white porcelain table on a riser, with a metal bucket, painted white, hanging below. A drain in the table funneled toward the bucket, and I could easily imagine what its purpose might be. Everything in the room was white, it seemed, except the floor, which had black represented, a result of being tiled in a classic checkerboard pattern. There was one person already in the room, busily arranging various instruments.

"Ah, Carl," Arenberg said, distaste evident in his voice. "You've gotten everything ready, I see."

"Yes, Mr. Arenberg," the man said, his voice thick with a German accent. It was difficult to determine his exact age, but he looked old. His head was almost completely bald on top, with a fringe of white hair around the sides and back. A white pointed beard jutted from his chin and round, metal-rimmed spectacles gave him a grandfatherly appearance, except he also gave off an unnerving air that I couldn't quite place.

"You really don't have to do this, you know," Arenberg said.

"It's no bother at all," the old man said. "I don't mind. Are you getting a body out now?"

"Yes. The Danby woman. Do you know where she is?"

The old man nodded and went to a row of doors in the wall, behind each of which, I assumed, lay a body waiting to be processed. He pointed to the second from the left and Arenberg moved forward.

"Give me a hand, will you, Wolfe," he said, opening the door and pulling out a gurney. On the gurney lay a form covered with a white sheet—Mrs. Danby. I started forward, but the old man beat me to it and grasped the gurney handle on the opposite side of Arenberg. Together, they transferred the body from the gurney to the white morgue table with the ghastly hanging bucket. The old man placed a small block of wood tenderly under the corpse's head, and then propped the now-empty gurney against the wall. Then he stood there awkwardly, his oddly long arms dangling and his head, balanced precariously on a pencil-thin neck, bobbing back and forth.

"You can go now, Carl," Arenberg said brusquely.

At first, I thought the old man was going to bow and back obsequiously from the room, but at last he turned smartly and marched through the double swinging doors and disappeared into the hall.

"He's a strange fellow," Arenberg said, staring after the old man. "Goes around calling himself 'Count,' but I don't think he's actually a count or has any title whatsoever. Works in radiology and occasionally assists with autopsies."

Arenberg turned to the body on the table and pulled

back the sheet with no sense of decorum. It was clear this man had seen many dead bodies, and the addition of one more made little difference. He bent close to the gaping throat wound, frowning. He picked up a scalpel from the tray of tools prepared by the old man and poked at the edges of the wound. After a few moments, he straightened and dropped the scalpel back onto the metal tray with a clatter.

"Well," he said, "I can tell it's a knife cut and that's about it. To be honest, I'm hoping this is a nice, simple suicide. I don't need a murder investigation right now."

"Mind if I take a look?"

He regarded me thoughtfully for a moment. "You know something about medical examination?"

"Not officially. My father wanted me to be doctor and so I took some courses on that track. But it wasn't for me. I dropped out quite early. Nonetheless, I did pick up a few things. That was around the time I developed an interest in criminology. I spent time around law enforcement and was present for more than one autopsy on the body of a violent crime victim."

"Well, then," Arenberg said, "you likely know more than I do on the topic. Take a peek and see if you can make anything out."

I stepped next to the body and, reaching across the dead woman's torso, retrieved a scalpel and forceps from the tray. With these instruments, I began to probe the outline of the wound, from one side to the other. I reached back a few years to my formative college days, trying to dredge up any nuggets from the pompous professors I disdained and hard-bitten detectives I wanted so badly to emulate. As I examined the wound, a picture began forming in my mind. I began speaking, more as a way of crystallizing it for myself rather than for Arenberg.

"Cut throat injury was present over anterior aspect of neck, margins clean at the head of the cut—no, both angles of injury were cleanly cut. Underlying cartilage, soft tissue, blood vessels, and musculature cut in a manner corresponding to the surface injury. Carotid artery on the right side incised; carotid on the left side spared. No tentative incisions present over the neck, slight tailing as wound progresses to victim's left side."

I stepped back and dropped the instruments onto the tray with a clatter loud enough to wake the dead in the room. I looked up at Arenberg to find him observing me with a good deal more respect than he had afforded me just moments before.

"I'd say you picked up a few things," he said.

"A few," I admitted. "I'm guessing if we were to ask Mr. Danby, he'd tell us his wife was right-handed."

"What difference does that make?"

"The deepest part of the wound is where it first begins. On Mrs. Danby, this is on her right side. A right-handed person cuts from left to right."

"And this cut runs right to left."

"Yes."

"It's worth checking into," Arenberg admitted. "Of course, if Mrs. Danby was left-handed, then it's back up for grabs."

"Not exactly," I said, pointing at the right side of Mrs.

Danby's throat. "The cut's deepest here, so we're safe in assuming that's where the cut began. It gets progressively shallower as the incision proceeds along the throat, but it never becomes hesitant and uncertain. It's a clean stroke."

"And this means what?"

"When people cut their own throats, there are a few tell-tale signs. Often, there are smaller cuts at the beginning of the wound, as the person makes a couple of experimental runs, but is stopped by the initial pain or perhaps uncertainty. Then, once they've made up their mind, they dig in deep and begin to draw the knife across. But the cut trails off quickly as the shock sets in. Rarely is there a cut that stretches entirely from side to side, and never one as clean as this."

"I'll have to take your word for it," Arenberg said. "I'm only coroner by virtue of my position as justice of the peace. Ex officio, they call that. Most of the time, we don't need an expert down here and I get along just fine. I won't admit to being happy with what you're telling me, though. Not to be hardhearted, but a suicide would have made my job a lot easier. As it is, we've got to open an investigation and things could be complicated. As I'm sure you know, Key West doesn't like complicated."

"Sorry to be the bearer of bad tidings," I said. "I'm just calling it the way I see it. I'm no expert either—not certified or anything."

Arenberg studied me for a moment. I could almost see the wheels turning in his head and wondered if he was weighing the pros and cons of ruling it a suicide regardless of my input. If he did, there'd be little I could do. He was a man well-known and well-liked in Key West. While I'd spent enough time here to be considered local, and was accepted as such, Arenberg's sphere of influence was a force to be reckoned with. And I could understand why he'd want to smooth it over. Suicides were just as scandalous as a murder, but much cleaner in terms of the law. Murders were...messy. And complicated.

The justice of the peace shrugged at last. "Well, there's nothing for it but to open it up to investigation. Maybe we'll get lucky and it'll be the husband. What's his name?"

"Mike."

"Mike, right. You two went to school together, didn't you?"

"That's right. Played football for Key West High. The Fighting Conchs."

Arenberg nodded thoughtfully. "Do you think he might have done it?"

"Mike's a hothead and a bit of a bum, mostly why we drifted apart out of school. That and the fact that I went to school in New England and he stayed here. But I have a hard time seeing him slitting his wife's throat. Too cold-blooded. Like I said, Mike's a hothead. A moment of passion, yes. Physical abuse in anger; now that I could understand. But this...I don't think he did it."

"That figures with what I know about Danby," Arenberg said. "Although I'll have to get more acquainted with him very soon. Any other thoughts?"

I opened my mouth to tell him about the prostitution, but something stopped me. I didn't know if I was protecting Mike, Mrs. Danby's posthumous reputation, or simply keeping my powder dry. Whatever the reason, I found myself closing my mouth again and shaking my head.

Arenberg look disappointed but didn't press the issue. "Danby still living over in that little second floor apartment of his?"

"Yeah. Been there ten years."

"I'll drop by and see him. Thanks for the help. You hear anything, you come to me, understand?"

I nodded and then understood I was being dismissed.

I walked out the swinging doors and passed the old man that Arenberg had called Carl. He recognized me and stopped me by placing a hand on my arm.

"The woman. She was murdered?"

"The jury's still out," I said, not wishing to share information with anyone I didn't know.

"A pity. A lovely thing." The old man let go of my arm and walked away down the hall, the jerky movements of his thin arms and legs reminiscent of a marionette.

I watched him for a moment, then turned and walked out into the crushing heat of the afternoon.

6

I sat in Delmonico's that evening, waiting for my date. She was running behind, but I wasn't worried. Tiki was always late. In fact, she was late so often that fifteen minutes past was now her idea of being on time. I checked my Bulova for the time. Tiki would argue about many things, but she never questioned my Bulova. I was in college when I heard the advertisement on the radio that announced, "At the tone, it's eight o'clock, Bulova Watch Time." From that moment on, I decided I had to have a Bulova watch, and ran down the next morning and put one on a layaway plan. Twenty dollars later, it was mine. It had been a steep price for a broke college kid, but it was still my most prized possession, next to my nickel-plated .38.

The front door of Delmonico's opened and Tiki breezed in, somehow looking cool and refreshing. Although the sun had already sunk, sizzling, into the ocean, the heat and humidity remained behind, less eager to abandon the island. I checked my watch. She was ten minutes late, which meant, of course, that she was five minutes early.

She slid into the chair across from me, smiling as she pointed at my watch. "How'd I do?"

"You're right on time," I said.

It was what I always said, because keeping Tiki happy was usually more important than starting an argument over a silly thing like time. I was also aware that most Conchs didn't share my opinion concerning the importance of time, a habit I'd picked up in the dubious civilization of New England. There, the clock was king. In Key West, time was more like a pawn, to be used as the islanders saw fit and for their own purposes, not to be mourned if lost. And Tiki was a Conch if there ever was one, having been born on the island and her birth announced by placing a conch shell on a stick outside her parents' house, open end up. She'd told me that her father, wishing to have a boy, had staked out the shell early and placed the point end up, hoping to influence the child's sex, but upon being informed by the doctor that it was a girl, had to shuffle out and turn the shell over under the watchful eyes of the neighbors. To my knowledge, Tiki had never even visited the Florida mainland and I doubted she wanted to.

"You're learning fast, Simon," she said, smiling, appreciating my laid-back response to her question. She took a menu and scanned it quickly, but I knew she'd be getting the same as she always did at Delmonico's: arroz con pollo and Spanish garbanzos. I opted for the same thing and motioned for the waiter. He took our order and then retreated back to the kitchen.

I smiled. "Not that fast. We've been seeing each other a year now."

"Has it been that long?"

"One year this week, as a matter of fact."

"It would have been longer if you hadn't run away to the States."

"Key West is part of the States."

"Depends on who you ask," Tiki said, smiling.

I almost took the bait by saying that Key West's status as a part of Florida wasn't a matter of opinion but saw the trap just in time. Key West was a world unto itself, the end of the line for many of its residents, and prided itself on independence and respect for the individual. It had enjoyed a thriving rum-running business during Prohibition, a government act viewed with wry amusement by the Key West populace, as enterprising seafarers imported booze from Cuba in the dark of night, dodging federales in the honorable pursuit of quenching local thirst. Prohibition had been repealed only four years prior, although the only change was that the drinking was now done more openly; it had never actually stopped in Key West.

I fixed Tiki with an appraising eye. She looked relaxed and certainly seemed in decent humor, but I felt she was spoiling for a fight, something that was not her natural inclination. She noticed my gaze and cocked an eyebrow.

"See something you like?"

"Always," I said.

"You're looking at me funny."

"Am I?"

"Don't play coy with me, Simon. Is something bothering you?"

"I was going to ask you the same question."

I expected her to reply with some attempt at humorous diversion, but she surprised me by looking down at the table. Her face had fallen, and she looked suddenly on the verge of tears. I leaned in and, reaching out, placed one of my hands over hers, which were now clasped together on the table top.

"You've heard about Mrs. Danby, I take it?"

I nodded. "Yes. But I didn't know you two were friends. Why has this upset you so badly?"

"Do you know what they're saying?"

I suspected that I did, but I wanted to hear it from her. "No, what?"

Tiki leaned in close and lowered her voice. "That she was a prostitute."

I tried my best to look surprised. "Where did you hear this?"

"From Susan."

"Susan Mayfield?"

Tiki nodded. "Her sister was the best of friends with Mrs. Danby."

"And she had no idea about Mrs. Danby's...work?"

"None. At least, that's what she told Susan. And I don't know why she would lie to her own sister."

"Everybody has a reason to lie," I said.

The waiter arrived with our food and we fell silent as the dishes were arranged on the table. When once more alone, Tiki picked up her fork and moved her food around. Her positive façade had faded somewhat.

"Something wrong?" I asked.

"Do you really believe that?"

"Believe what?"

"That everybody has a reason to lie."

"Yes."

More food shifting. "That's a depressing thought."

"You're forgetting who you're talking to," I said. "Everything I do is focused on the lies people tell. The investigations are obviously focused on that, but writing weaves the lives of fictional characters and discovers their motives. I suppose I've become conditioned to assume everyone has something to hide."

Tiki at last settled on a bite of chicken, speared it, and brought it to her mouth. As she chewed, she shook her head. "Not me," she said.

"Oh really? There's nothing in your life you'd rather be kept a secret?"

"No. I'm an open book."

I smiled. "I think you're a lot more complicated than you like to admit."

"What, you think I'm a foreign spy?"

"That would make our pillow talk even more interesting," I said. "But I should tell you now that I don't know any government secrets."

Tiki smiled back at me and adopted a mysterious, exotic accent. "My superiors will be most disappointed to hear this. I suppose I shall have to find a new American lover. One with more advantageous connections."

"You should be in the movies," I said, laughing. "But I suppose that would mean leaving Key West."

"Is it such a bad thing to stay in one place your whole life?"

"I suppose not, if you like where you're at."

"And I love it here."

"Of course," I said, "the only way to find out if you like somewhere else better is to go to other places."

"You did that. And you ended up back here."

I nodded. "Very true. Leaving was a good experience for me, though. There's something about only experiencing the familiar that keeps a person from being able to understand other people. I suppose it's simply a matter of seeing how other people live and think. It changes you. I remember going to a lecture by a well-known writer who'd served in the Great War. He was talking about how much he hated Germans—all Germans—and it wasn't until he met some by accident, on a place other than a battlefield, that he realized they were just like other people, and that he had more in common with them than not."

"Some people are saying there will be another war very soon," Tiki said. "Once more with Germany."

"Maybe so," I said, "but it won't be with the German people. They just want what everyone else wants: to live in peace and support their families. The Treaty of Versailles more or less guaranteed another war."

"Let's not talk politics," Tiki said. She frowned and then stabbed her chicken with increased aggression. "How is your writing going? Are you working on something new for me to read?"

"I've started and restarted the same thing at least a dozen times, but it won't go. I do have something exciting to tell you, though."

"Oh?"

"I had a chance meeting with Mr. Hemingway, and he asked to read something of mine."

Tiki's squeal of delight caused everyone in the restaurant to look at us. It was exactly the reaction I had hoped for, as I knew she was a fan of Hemingway's work, especially his book *A Farewell to Arms*, which she considered to be the best book in American literature, next to *The Adventures of Huckleberry Finn*.

"That's so incredible, Simon!" Her eyes had come alive and I couldn't help smiling at the sight of her happiness, particularly since I saw some pride in me showing through. "What did you give him? Has he read it yet? Did he like it? What did he say? Oh god, this is so exciting!"

"Calm down," I said, laughing. "It's not that big of a deal."

"Not a big deal? Not a big deal? Simon, this is Ernest Hemingway!"

"I know, I know. But you're acting like I met Henry James or something."

Tiki's face turned stormy, as I knew it would. "First of all, Henry James died twenty years go. And second, that was old stuff even while he was alive. Hemingway's style is still fresh, none of that pomp and circumstance for him. But what did he say?"

"He said he liked my story and that it showed promise.

He thought it could use a little cutting, but he seemed to think it was good."

If Tiki's smile got any wider, I feared it might split her face in two. I knew why she appeared so pleased. Her ongoing criticism of my writing was that it needed to be trimmed. "Take off the fat," she always said. "The reader doesn't need to know that." I always resisted, arguing that the reader didn't know me like she did and therefore couldn't be expected to guess my mind. In this case, however, she'd been proven right, and she was enjoying every second of it.

I shrugged, acting as if the whole thing was of small importance, setting her up for my big finish. "But I suppose he liked it well enough, because he invited me over to his house to watch some fights."

I thought at first Tiki was on the verge of having a stroke. She set her fork down hard on the plate, causing a loud clatter that would have been embarrassing, had I not been enjoying her reaction so much.

"You...went to his house?" she breathed.

"Yes," I said breezily. "We had drinks and then he asked me to box. We went a couple of rounds. I had an opening, but I let it pass and he belted me one. Knocked me out."

"You were knocked unconscious by Ernest Hemingway?"

I felt a triumphant laugh burbling up inside and had to struggle to keep it from bursting out in a braying guffaw. I could do nothing except nod as the hilarity detonated inside like a mortar shell, causing me some real concern that I might have sustained internal injuries. Suppressing such wild mirth was, it turned out, as dangerous as attempting to sneeze with one's eyes open.

"Pay the check," Tiki hissed.

"What?"

"Pay the check." Without waiting for my lead, Tiki hailed the nearest waiter, who, upon hearing her request, went to get our check. He was back moments later and I settled the bill. Then Tiki was out the door with me right behind her.

"What's the idea?" I said. "I wasn't done with my—"

My weak protest was cut off as she pressed her lips hard against mine, her fingers intertwining in the hair on the back of my head. Her body contoured with mine and I felt her firm breasts through the thin cotton of her dress. My arms went around her, and I placed one hand on her shoulder blades and the other on the small of her back, pulling her closer still. I felt the heat of her body and the slight dampness of her lower back as the heavy night air enveloped us in its own tropical embrace.

I heard a cascade of catcalls as an old car full of young people roared past, probably on their way to some remote part of the island to engage in their own type of "recreation."

"Your place or mine?" I said.

"Yours," she said.

We went to my place, a room I rented for a dollar per day. I had to fumble with the key, my fingers suddenly feeling the size of bowling pins, but at last the lock turned and we were inside, struggling toward the bed even as we began removing one another's clothing. The floor littered with garments, we fell, tangled together, onto the mattress, and made love on top of the sheets. It was fast, fierce sex, and within minutes, for the blink of an eye, rivers ran backward, and the tide reversed.

I rolled away and searched my bedside drawer for a stray cigarette, found one, and we alternately puffed. We were both breathing hard, sweating profusely, and periodically laughing aloud with the sheer joy of our intimacy.

"How was it for you?" Tiki asked between puffs.

"You couldn't tell?"

She grinned. "You seemed like you were having a good time."

"It's always good with you," I said, "although I don't know exactly how to feel about you getting frisky by learning I was decked by Hemingway. If I'd beaten him, now that I could understand."

"Maybe it's best if you don't think about it."

Tiki passed back the cigarette. She was still smiling, but I sensed a hint of melancholia seep into her demeanor. This wasn't unusual for her after sex, and I kept thinking I should ask her about it. But the time to talk about concerns with intercourse is not during sex or immediately thereafter, which was when I most noticed the vague sadness. In fact, there was no good time to talk about concerns with intercourse, unless a couple is on solid footing and has established a rapport about such things and a system for approaching delicate subjects. Tiki and I did not have that kind of relationship. I often wondered what, exactly, was the state of our connection. We clearly enjoyed one another's company and I knew I harbored romantic feelings for her beyond the sexual. Not love, perhaps, but certainly more than mere physical attraction. I could only guess at her feelings for me, for Tiki was loath to discuss matters of the heart. I'd found this disconcerting when I first noticed it, having been taught by both theory and practice that the average woman was usually the one more eager to delve into such matters. But I eventually made peace with the fact that Tiki was not the average woman, even going so far as to consider myself lucky to have found a woman who avoided any discussion of emotion. Then there were the times, such as when the sadness crept in, that I found her reticence more troubling.

I finished the cigarette and stubbed it out in the dark amber glass ashtray on the bedside table. I swung my legs off the bed and then rose to collect my clothes from the floor. As I gathered them, I felt Tiki's eyes on me.

"Are you going out?"

"Yeah," I said. "I thought I'd run down for a drink. You mind?"

"Do you want company?"

"Why don't you just relax and take a load off," I said. "You can stay here tonight if you're too tired to head back to your place." I dressed hurriedly, anxious to get out of the room to escape the daggers in her eyes. I could tell she was angry that I was going out alone, and normally, I would have welcomed her company, but I was hoping to get some leads on the Danby murder and always worked best alone.

"Fine," she said, her voice flat. "I hope you have a real good time." She grabbed a copy of *Life* from the bedside table and opened it with a snap. The large pages covered her entire face, making it clear she was through speaking with me for the evening. On the magazine's front cover, the black and white photograph of a 100-year-old woman smiled out at me, a cigarette held jauntily in her left hand via a pipe-style cigarette holder. The image seemed to hold some irony, considering Tiki's current mood, but instead of grappling with the esoteric, I finished securing my belt, stepped into my shoes, and left the room.

7

I originally intended to stop back into Sloppy Joe's but decided to try my luck elsewhere. I thought about Raul's over on the eastern side of the island, but I wasn't dressed for it and, besides, Tiki was upset enough without finding out I went to her favorite club without her. So instead, I headed to Thomas Street to Pena's Garden of Roses. I walked up onto the wide porch, between the tall, whitewashed support pillars, and into the building. I had to push myself inside, as the place was busy, and I saw Pena himself, a tiny little man with a pencil moustache, prominent ears, and a sharply receding hairline, skillfully navigating the sea of customers with a tray of assorted drinks. He wore a white tuxedo jacket with black pants and bowtie, somehow managing to appear comfortable in spite of the heat.

I ordered a beer and then began looking around at the faces of the drinkers. Most were regulars, although some I didn't know. I spotted a group of men at the back where they had moved together two of the rectangular tables. They were all drinking beer and it was clear they weren't on their first. They were laughing loudly, clapping each other on the back and generally having a riotous time. I made my way closer to listen. As I got closer, I could tell they'd just come from a sea expedition. They smelled of salt water and fish. They were so ripe, in fact, that I noticed other customers edging their own chairs and tables so as to widen the distance between themselves and the revelers.

And then I heard a familiar voice, rising above the rest, and realized it was Hemingway. His back was to me, but the big head and voice were unmistakable. He held his drink high. He was relating some tale and the others were leaning in, laughing wildly at nearly every sentence, whether it was a punchline or not.

"So he hooks this big marlin and practically lets go of the goddamn rod. If it hadn't been in the gimbal, the entire rig would've been gone in a second. Starts getting out of the chair, but yell at him, 'Father, get back in the goddamn chair or so help me I'll belt you, man of God or otherwise.' He sits back down, grabs the rod, and starts going at it with this fish. About an hour later, he's completely exhausted, wants to let it go. But I've seen the fish jump and it's a beauty—a goddamn record if it's a pound—so won't let him quit. A minute later, he's begging me to take over. 'Back's on fire,' he says, 'hands locked.' I say, 'Father, if two men take the same fish, won't count as a record.' He says he doesn't care. 'Record be damned,' he says. I'm shocked by the language, him being priest and all, but the sea does things to a man. I see he's about to drop dead, so take over and a half hour later, land the sonofabitch. Sure enough, record at one hundred nineteen and a half pounds."

By this time, I'd moved around the table enough to be in his line of sight. He saw me just as he ended his story and his face brightened with recognition.

"Look who it is," he said. "Pull up a chair, kid." To the others, he said, "The gumshoe was telling you about. Tracked a working girl right onto property. That's balls for you."

A chair had appeared before me and I lowered myself into it. Within moments, a drink was shoved into my hand that wasn't already holding the beer.

"Here on a case, Thin Man?"

"Could be," I said.

A man with slightly bulging eyes and a bald head, who was sitting on the far side of the table, leaned forward. "What's the case? If it's a case of scotch, we'll be happy to help."

Everyone but Hemingway laughed uproariously and even I had to smile, recognizing the line as something taken from the movie that had no doubt inspired Hemingway's reference to me as "Thin Man."

"The kid's okay," Hemingway said. "Took a straight punch from me and lived to tell about it. Isn't that right, Thin Man?"

The man who'd made the joke about scotch adjusted his thick glasses and blinked his protruding eyes, looking like a bullfrog hungry for flies. "You know, the Thin Man title wasn't the name of the detective in the movie. It was actually—"

"Can it, Dos," Hemingway said bluntly. "If going to be tedious, sit somewhere else."

The man called Dos closed his mouth and sat back in his chair, but I could tell he wasn't happy about it. I noticed an undercurrent of animosity between the two men that I had not expected. I knew the man called Dos to be John Dos Passos, the author of *42 Parallel*, which I had read, and two other books, *1919* and *The Big Money*, which I had not. I also knew he and Hemingway were friends, which was why the toxic interaction between the two men had caught me by surprise.

Hemingway turned back to me. "You on the Danby case?"

I nodded. "On behalf of the husband."

"I hear they like him for the job."

"They always like the husband," I said. "And more often than not, they're right."

"But not this time?"

"I don't think so."

The subject turned abruptly back to fishing and the drinking went on for another half hour. Then I felt my bladder demanding attention, so I stood up and made my way to the men's room. I'd just finished putting myself back together when I felt a hand on my shoulder. I turned to see Hemingway. I stepped away from the urinal.

"It's all yours," I said.

He stepped forward and, adopting a wide-legged stance, began relieving himself. He still held the drink in one hand. "Didn't want to say anything out there," he said.

"Anything about what?"

"About the woman."

"You mean Mrs. Danby."

"In light of certain things, should probably tell who she was hanging around at my place. Don't want to go to cops —they don't see the angles. Thought you might be more discreet."

"Who was it?"

"Guy named Morales. He's sitting at the table now. Big guy, Cuban. Tight with Josie Russell over at Sloppy Joe's. Supplied with rum during Josie's speakeasy days."

"And you think he might have had something to do with Mrs. Danby's murder?"

"Not for me to say, kid. That's your racket. Only reason I'm telling you is because I think you'll play it smart. The cops—they'd pin it on him fast just to close the file. Nothing else, he might give you a lead."

"Thanks, Mr. Hemingway. I appreciate your trust."

"Don't mention it, kid. And enough with the Mr. Hemingway. Call me Papa. Everyone does."

"Okay—Papa."

Hemingway grinned, pleased with the sound of it. "Better get back to drinking. Leaving soon for the mainland, then New York, then Spain. Going to cover war for the North American Newspaper Alliance. Might not be back for a while. With any luck, will bag a couple fascists for good measure."

"See you when you get back," I said.

"Keep your nose clean, kid."

He left the restroom and I followed him out. I tried to settle my tab but was informed it had already been taken care of. I looked back and saw Hemingway watching me. He nodded and raised his glass. I nodded back and then left the bar, wondering if I'd ever see him again. Spain was a dangerous place to be, and if I knew anything about Hemingway, I knew he'd find his way to the frontlines or die trying.

I wasn't ready to throw in the towel—or ready to face Tiki's cold wrath—so I detoured up to Sloppy Joe's, which I knew to be Mike's favorite hangout, both before and after it changed locations. If there was going to be a night when he'd be out drinking, this would be it.

I wasn't disappointed. Mike sat in the corner, alone, a bottle of scotch on the table. His head was bowed, and he held his glass, swirling it around and around, watching the liquid's amber vortex. He was the very picture of a rock bottom rummy. I pulled out a chair and sat down. He didn't raise his head, but somehow knew it was me.

"It's a hell of a thing, Sims," he said. "A hell of a thing."

"It sure is, Mike," I said, assuming he was talking about the murder.

"Used to be I could come in here and never drink alone. Now look at me. I might as well have leprosy the way these clowns are keeping their distance."

I looked around. It was true. The place was hopping, but there was a conspicuous vacuum around Mike's table.

"At first, they didn't even want to let me buy the bottle. Can you believe that?"

"Sorry, Mike. Nobody knows what to think."

"What do you think? You think I did it?"

I reached over, picked up the bottle, and took a pull. "No, Mike. I don't."

"I wish I knew if you were telling me the truth."

"I'm sitting here, aren't I? It's my reputation too."

"Quite an accomplishment when you get too disreputable even for a place like Key West."

"Like you say, Mike. It's a hell of a thing." I knew by now that his statement had been less about the murder and more about the bar patrons' treatment of him, but I was trying to refocus his anger. "It's not every day a woman around here gets her throat cut clean through."

Mike drained his glass and refilled it. "Yeah. I guess not."

"Take New York City. You'd probably be a celebrity by now. All the press wanting to get your story."

"I've never been to New York City."

"You might like it."

"Doubt it. Besides, I'm not supposed to leave town, remember?"

"If you didn't do it, you've got nothing to worry about."

"I wish I could believe that too. They'll pin it on me, Sims. You know they will. They need a fast fall guy and I'm it."

"Not if I can help it. You got a lawyer?"

"Not yet."

"Get one. See Louis Harris. He's the best defense attorney around here."

"If I could afford an attorney, Thelma might not have found it necessary to—" Here Mike broke off and began to sob.

I looked around, uncomfortable, and then stretched out a hand and patted him awkwardly on the shoulder. "You couldn't have known," I said, although I had no idea how he couldn't have known.

"I should've been a better husband," Mike sobbed. "I was a real sonofabitch, Sims. A real sonofabitch."

"Come on, Mike. Have a drink. You can't change what's done."

"All I wanted was to live the good life. Always on me to get a job. I thought she was just a nag, but a woman needs things, you know? I never brought her flowers once, Sims. Not once. She bought a new dress and I hit the roof. Made her take it back. Humiliated her. I was a real sonofabitch, Sims. I deserve to be locked up. I might as well have killed her." His voice was rising and attracting attention.

"Mike," I said. "You need to get hold of yourself. Think about what you're saying. Come on, let's get out of here and head back to your place. We can take the rest of the bottle."

"My place? You know how many ghosts are at my place, Sims? It even smells like her. I can see her everywhere in there."

Someone approached the table, pulling a chair along with them. They began sitting down and I turned to let the guy have it when I saw it was Brucie. I never thought I'd be happy to see him, but right that moment, I could have hugged his neck like a father welcoming home the prodigal son.

"Hey, you gotta keep it down, Mike," Brucie said. "Folks

are lookin' at ya. You don't want them callin' the cops, do ya?"

These surprisingly sensible words somehow made it through the fog of grief and alcohol in Mike's brain. He nodded, and I saw the wind go out of his sails. He sat back, still nodding. He reached for his glass, missed, tried again, and this time managed to hold on to it long enough to get it to his lips. He slurped at it, a rivulet of scotch running out the corner of his mouth and onto the front of his white cotton shirt.

"You two fellas are the only pals I've got left," Mike said. His speech had begun to slur more noticeably in just the time I'd been at his table and his eyelids were growing heavy. The intense emotion, with its passing, had ushered in exhaustion.

"How long's he been at the bottle?" Brucie asked.

I shrugged. "I just got here." And then I saw Mike slide sideways. "Watch out, he's going down."

Mike knew he was falling, but his equilibrium was too sodden to be trusted. He gripped the edge of the table but only succeeded to pushing outward, speeding his descent. Before either Brucie or I could reach him, Mike's big body hit the floor with a thud.

8

I woke up the next morning in my hotel room, sitting in a chair and leaning across the table with my arms crossed under my head as a pillow. My mouth was dry and tasted like old leather. I raised my head and looked around. Sun was streaming in through the window and somebody was rattling the doorknob. I felt for my .38, then saw it on the table about a foot from my right hand. I'd just grasped the handle when the door opened and Tiki walked in, carrying a little tray with an assortment of breakfast items. She walked over and set the tray on the table.

"You don't deserve it, but I thought you could use something to eat. And your friend definitely needs it."

"My friend?"

"Yeah. Mike Danby."

I rubbed my eyes, trying to orient myself to the current state of affairs. "What's this about Mike?"

For the first time, I became aware of light snoring coming from the direction of the bed. I looked over and saw Mike lying across the bed, his long legs hanging off the side. He was still fully dressed, except for his shoes, which had been removed and carelessly flung across the room.

"What's he doing here?"

"That's what I asked last night," Tiki said.

And then it came back to me. Mike at Sloppy Joe's, him passing out dead drunk, and hauling him to my place—because it was closer than Mike's apartment and Mike was a heavy bastard. I also remembered Tiki's reaction to being awakened by three guys—me, Mike, and Brucie—with one dead drunk and the other two not exactly sober. I also remembered Tiki surprising me by being remarkably calm about the whole thing. At least, she hadn't screamed or thrown anything. And now she'd brought juice and rolls. I reached out for a glass of orange juice and swigged it back. The acidity cut through the stale alcohol film from the night before, leaving me feeling fresher and much improved. Half a sweet roll later, I felt halfway human.

I pointed at Mike's sleeping form. "Suppose I should wake him, huh?"

"It's your room," Tiki said. There was just the slightest hint of an edge in her voice that let me know I wasn't completely off the hook. Perhaps she'd only called a truce until the current crisis had abated.

While still waging an internal struggle concerning the benefits and drawbacks of rousting a man sleeping off a night of heavy drinking, the decision was made for me. There was a loud bang at the door and the sound caused a loud snort from Mike, which in turn brought him back into the land of the living.

"What the—?" He sat straight up, his head turning as if on a swivel. Then his face creased with pain as the harsh reality of his situation hit him like a sledgehammer. He grabbed his head in both hands and let out a howl worthy of the damned. He fell back onto the bed, covering his eyes and moaning. "It's bright—too bright—turn off the damn lights—oh my god, my head's pounding like a drum."

Tiki went forward and held out a glass of juice. "Here. Drink this."

Mike struggled to sit up, finally managed it, and took the glass. He sipped at it tentatively, grimacing as he did so. "A little hair of the dog would be better."

"Just drink it," Tiki said, playing the part of longsuffering nurse to the hilt.

There was another bang outside, this fainter and more muffled. Mike scowled in the general direction of the noise.

"It's the paper boy," I explained. "He makes it a matter of pride to hit the door of his customers with as much force as possible when he throws the papers." I went to the door, opened it, and bent down to get my copy of the *Key West Citizen*. As I was straightening up, another bang sounded from down the row of doors. I looked over and saw Jimmy, the paper boy, reaching into his sack for another folded paper missile.

"Hey, Jimmy!" I called out. "Been working on that arm, I take it?"

The kid glanced back. "Sure have, Mr. Wolfe. If I wanna pitch for the Yankees, I'll have to be in tip-top shape!"

I raised my hand. "Throw me a curve, kid."

Jimmy grinned, took the sack of papers from his shoulder, and assumed a pitcher's stance. He adjusted the bill of his cap, spat on the ground, then drew back and delivered a blistering strike right past my outstretched hand and through the window of the adjoining room. There was a squawk of surprise and annoyance from inside the room, followed by a long string of cursing.

"Get lost, kid!" I called out. "I'll deal with it."

Jimmy waved his thanks and made like a jackrabbit down the row of rooms, tossing papers as he went in a quick staccato: *whap whap whap.* I went to the broken window and leaned near the jagged hole where the paper had smashed through the glass.

"Sorry about the window, Mr. Gleason. Just have the manager charge it to my room."

The curtain jerked back, and the moist, pudgy face of the occupant glowered out at me.

"Ah, Wolfe. I should have known. A little early to be carousing, don't you think?"

"A little early to be a bastard, don't you think?"

"Bah!" The curtain fell back, and I heard the sound of the room telephone being yanked from its cradle. "Get me the manager!" Gleason yelped.

I returned to my room, wondering how I was going to pay for the window and why the people who needed murdering were never the ones who actually got murdered. No sooner had I walked into the room than the phone rang.

"Well, that was quick," I said.

Mike was plugging his ears, all the recent noise apparently threatening to split his head in two. I yanked the receiver off the side of the candlestick-style phone and put it to my ear.

"Wolfe's room," I barked into the mouthpiece.

"This is Frank Arenberg. Have you seen this morning's paper?"

"Just got it. Why?"

"Take a look."

I put the ear piece on the bedside table and unrolled the paper. The headline hit me right between the eyes: BODY MISSING FROM MORGUE.

"Are you looking at it?" Arenberg said.

"Yeah."

"Care to guess whose body is missing?"

I glanced over at Mike. He still had his ears plugged. "Mrs. Danby's?"

"What?"

"Mrs. Danby's?" I repeated, as loudly as I dared.

"Right the first time. Get over to Marine Hospital as soon as you can."

I hung up the ear piece. To Tiki, I said, "Gotta go. Try to keep Mike from reading any papers until I get back."

"What's happened?"

I flashed her the front page and then rolled up the paper. Mike took the fingers out of his ears.

"Has the war ended?" he moaned.

"For now," I said. "Just take it easy. I have to go out for a while, but I'll be back. If you need anything, Tiki can help. You should probably stay out of the sun until you get rehydrated and start feeling better. It's going to be a hot one."

FIVE MINUTES LATER, I was at the hospital and found Arenberg waiting for me on the front steps. I wouldn't go so far as to say he looked sick, but he clearly wasn't feeling his best.

"Can you believe this?" he growled.

"Not really," I said, being completely honest. "How does something like this happen?"

"With hospital staff being careless, that's how. Of course, I'm getting the blame for it. The news has already reached the mainland. I've been dodging phone calls from the Capital all morning."

"Why does Tallahassee care?"

"It's bad advertising. This is just the sort of thing that hits the wires hard and spreads fast."

"The *Citizen* got it quick."

"Blind luck on their part. They had a reporter at the hospital getting fifty stitches in his leg when an attendant realized the body was missing. Reporter jumps off the table and hobbles to the phone to call it in. About bled to death by the time they got him back on the table to finish sewing him up."

"Any leads on how—or why—the body was taken?"

"An officer went by to question the husband, but he wasn't at home. I figure he might have made off with the body and skipped town."

"Danby's at my place sleeping off a bender."

"You with him last night?"

I nodded. "I drank a bit myself, but I would have

remembered if we broke into the morgue and stole a body."

"Yes, I suppose you would. Well, there goes that idea. Nothing can be easy, can it, Wolfe?"

"Doesn't seem that way."

"And me with a full docket. That's one reason I wanted to see you."

"To complain about your workload?"

"I can do that by myself. No, I was thinking you could expand your investigation a bit."

"I don't follow you."

"You're looking into the murder of Mrs. Danby, aren't you?"

"On behalf of the husband, yes."

"Then why not do the same work for two employers? You'd get paid twice."

I frowned. "Why do I feel as if there might be strings attached to this?"

"No strings. I'd just want to be the first to know of any developments in the case."

"Why not let the police handle it?"

"Oh, they'll be working on it," Arenberg said. "But you know how it can be around here when the police get involved. Now, you—people know you. And think highly of you. You could stick your nose into places where an officer might get it cut off."

"You still like Mike Danby for the murder, don't you?"

"I'm not ruling it out. And neither should you. By being on the court's payroll, you'd be clear to investigate Danby along with any other suspects that might show up."

I didn't like the idea. In a way, I felt as if this would be a betrayal of Mike's trust. Of course, if he were guilty of murdering his wife, I wouldn't cover for him whether I was an acting officer of the court or not. On the other hand, the way Arenberg was presenting the proposal felt as if he was asking me specifically to investigate Mike—and to build a case against him. Then again, while Arenberg was right that an official investigator would have some doors closed to him, other doors would likely open, such as city resources and files.

"I'll do it on one condition," I said.

"And that is?"

"That I get the same courtesy that I extend to you. By that I mean information turned up by the police. I want to be the first to know of developments."

Arenberg stared at me for a long minute. At last, he nodded and stuck out his hand. "Done." He then cleared his throat and adjusted his suit. "Well, then. I'm needed at the courthouse. I'll let the proper individuals know that you're working for me, so you won't have trouble getting access and information. I'll also give you this." He removed a card from his pocket and then scribbled his signature on the back. He handed the card to me. "That should give you access about wherever you need to go. And, of course, I expect you'll be wanting to look over the morgue for any clues the body snatcher may have left behind."

I nodded.

"Very well, then."

We stepped inside the hospital and Arenberg flagged down a stout, middle-aged woman wearing a white nurse's uniform.

"Mrs. Garrity, this is Simon Wolfe, an investigator working for the court. I'd be obliged if you'd give him any assistance he may need."

Mrs. Garrity nodded curtly. Arenberg nodded his thanks, then turned and left the hospital. I turned to the nurse.

"Mrs. Garrity, is it?"

"Yes, Mr. Wolfe. I'm the head nurse here at Marine Hospital."

"Very good. I'd like to see the morgue, please."

She turned on her heel and walked away down the hall, her heels clacking loudly in quick staccato on the tile floor. Assuming I was expected to follow, I scrambled after her, finding to my surprise that I had to hurry to keep up with her. I wondered how someone with such short legs could cover so much ground, finally assuming it came from years of bustling around hospital corridors.

Soon we were at the same set of swinging doors as yesterday and there Mrs. Garrity left me. Without a word, she clacked away, arms moving like piston rods, leaving me standing alone. I reached out, pushed the doors open, and stepped inside. I wasn't thrilled to be alone in a room full of dead bodies and so it was with a surprising level of relief that I saw Carl in the room, busily cleaning the examination table. He looked up as I entered, and his bald head bobbed in recognition.

"Good morning," I said. "You're at it bright and early."

"Ah, yes," he said. "I am always happy to help at the hospital."

"I understand you're a radiologist. Do they always make the radiologists do a janitor's work?"

"I don't mind. It keeps me busy and helps the hospital run smoothly."

"Very thoughtful of you. Were you on duty last night?"

His head bobbed again. "I was, yes."

"Were you in the morgue at all?"

He paused in thought, stroking his white beard. "Only briefly and just once."

"And did you see anything suspicious?"

"No, no. Everything was quiet when I left."

I walked to the row of doors in the wall. "Do you mind showing me where Mrs. Danby's body was kept?"

He came forward, his thin body leaning forward as if he was walking into a stiff wind. He pointed at one door, then at another. "It was here—wait, no—this one. Yes, this one."

I reached out and tried the handle. The door opened easily. I peered in. Inside was a metal slab. It was, of course, empty.

"Are these doors normally kept locked?" I asked.

"No. There is no way to lock them."

"Is there a handle on the inside?"

"No, sir."

"So it would be impossible to get out from the inside if the door was fully closed?"

He nodded.

"But, of course, there would be no reason for anyone to be on the inside. Unless they were dead."

"Correct, sir."

"What was your name again?"

"Carl. Carl Tanzler."

"Arenberg told me you're a count of some kind?"

His head bobbed once more. "Count Carl Tanzler von Cosel, yes. During my childhood in Germany, I had visions of my ancestor, Countess Anna Constantia von Cosel, who revealed to me the story of my heritage."

I regarded Tanzler with the same suspicion that I might have afforded a man who'd announced that he had married his dog, but he didn't seem to notice. I took one more look inside the empty chamber and then closed the door and stepped back.

"And you saw nothing suspicious last night."

"Nothing at all. Of course, I wasn't in the morgue for long."

"And the morgue doors—are they kept locked?"

Tanzler shook his head. "Never."

"Isn't that a bit unusual?"

He shrugged his bony shoulders. "Perhaps, but before last night, it was never considered necessary. After all, who would want to rob a morgue? It is only corpses. No valuables are kept here. Anything on the bodies is removed and kept in the hospital safe until claimed by relatives or the police."

For all his apparent nuttiness, I had to admit that Tanzler had a point. Who would want to rob a morgue? Was there something about the body I had missed? Some telltale clue that the killer wanted to remain a secret? I had focused my examination on the wound to the throat, ignoring the rest of the body. I silently cursed myself for lack of experience. A more seasoned detective would have checked over the entire corpse. And now it was too late. Even if the body were found, it would decompose quickly outside the cooling environment of the morgue. The heat and humidity would soon make any meaningful examination impossible.

"Well, then, I guess that's all I can do here," I said. "Thanks for the help. If you think of anything, any detail you might have forgotten, contact me. Here's my card." I reached into my pocket, feeling around for one of my hand-lettered calling cards—printing was a luxury I couldn't yet afford. I found one, which I handed over to Tanzler. He took it, read it, and slipped it into his breast pocket.

"I will certainly do that, Mr. Wolfe. And I hope you find the man who killed Mrs. Danby. A horrible thing."

"Horrible indeed, Carl. Horrible indeed."

9

After asking around at two other bars, I found Morales at Pepe's Café, the same eatery where Mrs. Danby had given me the slip. He seemed smaller than he had the previous night at the Garden of Roses, although that was probably because he appeared to be nursing a hangover with a cup of thick Cuban coffee, an espresso made from roasted Cuban coffee beans and dosed with a generous helping of sugar. He hunched over the cup, his shoulders forward and his eyes mere slits. He barely stirred when I slid into the booth.

"Mr. Morales?"

He grunted and squinted at me with eyes puffy from a late night of carousing.

"Do you have a few minutes to talk?"

Another grunt.

"It won't take long."

"Talk? You want to talk?" His eyes opened wider, and suddenly, he seemed bigger again. The eyes were black like a snake's, cold and expressionless. Even under the weather, he was obviously a dangerous man.

"If you can spare the time."

"Does it look like I'm doing anything, *pendejo*?"

"You make an excellent point," I said, shifting nervously. "Good, then. I'd like to talk about Thelma Danby."

"Who?"

"Thelma Danby. The woman who was murdered."

"That *puta*. I don't know nothing about her."

"You seem to know she was a whore. Or were you simply speaking in general terms?"

Morales scowled, although I wasn't sure if the reaction was for my benefit or just a symptom of his hangover. "Who are you, *idiota*? What do you want from me?"

I felt pleased that my status had improved from *pendejo* all the way up to *idiota* but didn't think I should make too much of it. He was quite possibly simply off his game.

"I would like to know when you saw Mrs. Danby last."

"What makes you think I knew the *mujer* at all?"

It was an astute question for a man in his condition and one I'd hoped somehow to avoid. I had no desire to betray any confidence Hemingway may have placed in me by telling me of Morales' dalliances with Mrs. Danby.

"I have my sources," I said, hoping the vague and cryptic explanation would satisfy his suspicion. Mentioning Hemingway's name would certainly be the fastest way to open what had thus far been a rather strained conversation, but I had no desire to burn any bridges.

"Sources, huh." Morales drank from his coffee cup. "And just who are these sources?"

"I'm not at liberty to say. But they are reliable and know that you had some...dealings with Mrs. Danby in a... professional capacity."

Morales grinned in spite of his sickly state. "'Professional capacity,'" he said. "I like that. *¡Es muy divertido!*"

"I'm glad it amuses you. So, when did you see her last?"

The Cuban drew himself up in his chair and squared his shoulders, instantly becoming the large, intimidating figure from the night before. "I broke no laws."

I didn't bother to correct him, because I knew what he meant. The difference between illegality and prosecution was broader here than on the mainland. In Morales' mind, he had done nothing wrong, either morally or legally, particularly being from Cuba, where prostitution was not only legal but often guarded by funded police protection.

"This isn't about the law," I said. "Any business arrangements you made with Mrs. Danby are of no concern to me. I'm interested only in finding her murderer."

"You are *policía?*"

I shook my head.

"Then why do you care?"

I hesitated, then said, "I am working for Mr. Danby. He only wants to know who killed his wife. Nothing more. Anything you can tell me would be most appreciated."

Morales drank his coffee and looked at me. I could see his brain working, trying to figure the angles. Then he nodded. "Very well. I knew her."

"When did you see her last?"

"Two nights ago."

"And everything seemed normal then?"

"Normal?"

"Did she say anything that made you think she was at all frightened?"

"No. Nothing."

"Did she ever mention any other men?"

"We never spoke of it. Even with *putas*, a man likes to believe he is the only one, even though we know that is not true."

"Did you know any of the others?"

"We never spoke of it."

"Do you know any reason why someone would kill her?"

Morales' face darkened. "Who can know why some men do what they do? Perhaps it was a jealous lover. Perhaps it was over money. Or perhaps a man with *una esposa* at home wanted to make sure no one would ever know of his transgression."

"Did you know the body has disappeared from the hospital morgue?" As I said this, I watched Morales closely, but he was either genuinely shocked or was an actor worthy of immediate contractual engagement.

"*¡Venga, no lo creo!*"

"It's true," I said. "You can see it in the paper."

"A body is a sacred thing!"

"Maybe now you can see why I am so eager to find the murderer. If I find who killed her, I might be able to find out who took the body as well."

"I wish I could help you," Morales said, "but I know nothing more than what I have already told you."

"And you're certain you don't know any other men who spent time with Mrs. Danby?"

Morales shifted in his chair, the first time I'd seen him truly uncomfortable. "I have heard of others, but none that would commit the horrible crimes you speak of. If I thought any of them were responsible, I would tell you."

I reached into my pocket and pulled out another of my hand-lettered cards. I handed it to Morales. At this rate, I was going to have to spend a couple of hours replenishing my stock.

He studied the card carefully. "Wolfe," he said. "I have heard the name."

"You'll call me if you hear anything or happen to remember any details that could help with my investigation?"

"I will call."

I slid out of the booth and stood up. "And I have your word?"

Morales made the sign of the cross. "*En la tumba de mi madre.*"

"Good enough," I said.

Outside, the sun was climbing higher and the heat was climbing right along with it. The bodega where I'd gotten the bollos wasn't far, and I decided that a cool Pepsi-Cola would suit me fine. I went inside and grabbed a drink out of the ice chest. Then I dropped a coin onto the counter, nodded in response to a muttered *gracias* from the elderly woman behind the counter, and walked back outside.

I was popping the top off the cola, when a Cuban boy ran up behind me.

"Señor!"

I turned around just in time to avoid being bowled over. "Whoa, hold it, there, kid. Where's the fire?"

"It is Señor Hemingway."

"What, did he die?"

"No, he wishes you to meet him at the docks."

"Now?"

"Si, señor."

I felt a little irritated at being summoned, but my curiosity quickly overcame any sense of annoyance. "He is at the Bight?"

The boy shook his head. "No, señor. The Navy yard."

I had to chuckle. It was just like Hemingway to dock his boat in restricted naval waters. This I had to see. "Okay, kid. Let's go see what the great man wants now."

Like everywhere in Key West, the naval dockyard wasn't far away and soon I saw a boat bobbing on the water next to a pier, with several men scurrying around. As I walked down the pier, I saw Hemingway standing atop his boat. He was clad in stained shorts and ragged shirt, looking like any run-of-the-mill deckhand. He spotted me and gave out a hearty halloo.

"What do you think of accommodations?" he asked, gesturing widely.

I climbed aboard with a helping hand from the man I'd recognized last night as John Dos Passos. "Is your boat now an official naval vessel?"

"Not yet," he said, "though pressing her into wartime service would be a hell of a time. Thompson, from down at the hardware, got me the okay to dock here. Nearer home than the Bight. You've not been on the *Pilar* before, have you?" He said this as though we'd been friends for years and the occasion of my maiden visit was from mere oversight and not a complete lack of opportunity.

"No, I haven't. She's a fine-looking vessel."

"That she is. Tried one just like her in '34 when I stopped out at Wheeler Shipyard. Had to have one. So I went by Arnold Gingrich—"

"From *Esquire*," a voice cut in. It was Dos Passos, standing directly behind me and listening in to the conversation.

Hemingway glowered. "Kid's a writer, Dos. He knows who Arnold Gingrich is. Don't you, Thin Man?"

I nodded, which was a straight-up lie. I'd never heard the name and, I was embarrassed to admit even to myself, I had never read *Esquire*.

"So I went by Arnold Gingrich," Hemingway continued forcefully, "and got three grand for some short pieces and made that a down payment on the *Pilar*. Can't say Pauline was thrilled but felt better when named it after her."

"Pilar is a nickname for Pauline," Dos Passos interjected.

In the blink of an eye, Hemingway came down from the flying bridge and grabbed Dos Passos by the shirt front. Hemingway's face was nearly purple as he came nose-to-nose with his friend.

"You popeyed pilot fish, who told you to talk? Shut your damn mouth before I stuff it full of bait! I've got half a mind to throw you off this boat right now, and if we were far enough out to sea, I just might!"

Dos Passos blinked his wide eyes, trying to back away from the verbal onslaught. At last, Hemingway released the man's shirt front and pushed him away. Then he turned on his heel and stalked back up to the bridge. A moment later, he shouted down to a crewman,

"You blow out the engine compartment?"

The crewman responded in the affirmative.

"Then let's take her out!"

An engine roared and I felt the boat come alive under my feet.

"Come on up to the bridge, Thin Man," Hemingway called down. "The view's terrific."

Avoiding eye contact with the humiliated Dos Passos, I made my way up to the flying bridge, where Hemingway was gripping the railing and grinning out at the sparkling sea. There was no trace of the anger from mere moments before, and all that remained was the sheer joy of a man in his element. Minutes later, the *Pilar* had entered open water and the engine was opened up

"She's a thirty-eight-footer," Hemingway said. "Had a couple improvements made. A fish well to keep the catch fresh and a wooden roller to help with hauling the fish on board. Lowered the transom. Got bigger fuel tanks than standard. Two motors on her. One a seventy-five horse-power for going places and a smaller one for trolling. You ever fish?"

"Just from the docks," I said. "I'm afraid I never got the chance to be aboard a fishing craft."

"Then today's your lucky day, Thin Man. You're going to fish today."

The boat looped and headed for the Gulf Stream, and I felt a knot start in my stomach. I was not an experienced fisherman, and if we were headed to the Stream, then Hemingway intended to make a serious catch. I remembered his story from the night before about the record fish and felt my palms get moist.

"While we go, let's get you geared up," Hemingway said, leading the way down to the deck. He glanced back and treated me to his broad, irresistible smile. "And don't worry. Been told am a damn good teacher."

I didn't find this particularly comforting, since it wasn't a simple failure that had me worried; it was failure in front of Hemingway. I hadn't even dredged up the courage yet to call him Papa as he'd requested, and now I was expected to butcher a sport at which he'd become something of an authority. The thought crossed my mind to precede Dos Passos overboard but that being out of the question, I resigned myself to whatever humiliation awaited me.

Hemingway got me suited with a fishing harness and began giving me pointers on the best way to land big fish. But I was too worried to comprehend most of what he was saying.

Along the way to the Stream, we ran alongside a long string of sargassum, yellowish-brown sea weed that can string for miles on the ocean surface. Sargassum also provides a suitable environment for various sea creatures. One of the other men on the boat, to whom I had yet to be introduced, grabbed a pole from where it lay near the cabin and used it to pull a clump of the weed onto the green-painted deck. He bent, picked up the weed, and shook it violently. Instantly, his feet were surrounded by tiny shrimp that jumped and skittered. The man calmly picked up the shrimp one by one and popped them whole into his mouth, chewing noisily. My stomach turned, but the man was obviously enjoying his impromptu meal. He saw me watching and my face no doubt showed my disgust because he smirked and then opened wide to show off the partially chewed contents of his mouth. I turned away, now more disgusted by the man himself than his nause-ating meal choice.

At last, but all too soon, Hemingway pushed me toward the wooden fishing chair. It had three wooden slats for the back and curved armrests. Protruding from the front was a metal-reinforced, concave wooden foot brace, giving it the look of an economy barber's chair. I sat down and posi-tioned myself so the gimbal, also built into the chair, was visible between my legs. Hemingway fitted the butt of the pole into the gimbal.

I motioned to my harness. "What do I need this for?"

"Don't want to go aboard," Hemingway said, using a metal clasp to connect the harness to the chair.

I swallowed hard. "Overboard?"

"Some of these fish will do it," he said. "Don't want to risk you being caught off guard, being a greenhorn. Not that there's anything wrong with that," he added. "We all had a first time."

I waited for the inevitable virginity joke, but Hemingway was now dead serious. I could see that, for him, fishing was no laughing matter. The others on the boat were not quite so reverential, however, and their festive attitudes had only increased as we'd motored our way to the Stream. I knew their high spirits were buoyed by the consumption of a bottle of Cuban rum someone had produced.

Hemingway scowled. "Damn lucky if we catch anything with the racket these boys are making."

I expected him to quiet them, and he could have with merely a word. Not only were we sailing on his boat, making him the undisputed captain of the voyage, but I knew there wasn't a man jack aboard who would question his authority. Most of these men were members of what was wryly referred to as "Hemingway's Mob," and they wanted to stay that way. But Hemingway held his peace as the *Pilar* slowed and turned to the less powerful trolling motor.

I sat in the chair and my concern gradually faded. It was my first time out, I reasoned, making the odds of catching anything truly challenging quite low indeed. The smell of salt water, the luscious breeze, and the expanse of sparkling water were slowly lulling me into having a pleasant time.

And then the fish took the line.

At first, I had no idea what was happening or why the entire crew let out a wild shout. All I knew was that the rod was bent and straining, and the line was whirring as it paid out.

"Alive, kid, look alive!" It was Hemingway, leaning over my shoulder. I glanced over and saw his dark, intense eyes fixed on the line where it disappeared into water. "You got a customer!"

I grabbed the pole and was about to hit, when Hemingway gripped my shoulder.

"Not yet," he grated out, his teeth clenched with excitement. "Not yet. He's just playing with you, Thin Man. Don't fall for his dirty tricks. Come on, come on—loosen the drag, kid."

"But shouldn't I—?"

"Patience, now. Give him room."

The line was zipping along, paying out in spades as the fish made his getaway.

"Now?" I asked.

"Steady…steady…may not have struck, just gripping the hook in his mouth."

Then, just when I thought I wouldn't be able to take it any longer, Hemingway shouted, "Hit him now, hit him good!"

I braced my feet and tightened the drag. The rod made an impossible bend and the line sang like a harp string. But the fish kept moving.

"Again, kid. Hit him again. Make him feel it this time, now."

I hit again, and this time, I felt an unspeakable weight on the line. "I've got him," I shouted, beside myself with the thrill of it. "I've hooked him!"

"That's great, kid, now easy. Now that the hook's set, don't want to open the set too wide or may throw it when he jumps."

"Will he jump?"

"He'll jump."

And sure enough, within seconds, the surface of the

ocean rose like a giant bubble for one split moment and then the largest broadbill I'd ever seen rose majestically skyward like an aeroplane climbing straight up. The sun flashed off the sides of the beautiful fish as the water poured over and down its purple-blue back and off the silver underbelly. The sword seemed to pierce the dome of the sky and then the fish was falling back down, the curved tail slicing into the roiling water below—and then it was gone. The rod swung back and vibrated in my hands, and the line went slack. A groan went up from the crew. Hemingway cursed and straightened. I thought I might throw up.

"Don't worry about it, kid," Hemingway said, lightly punching my shoulder. "If you'd have caught a fish that big on your first time in the chair, might have had to kill you anyway."

After the disappointment with the broadbill, the fishing dried up. The men began getting frustrated and that frustration soured the liquor in their bodies so that they began turning ugly and mean. The longer we went without a hit, the uglier and meaner they got.

We had a late lunch of boiled eggs, cheese, and hard Cuban bread, washing it all down with an excellent red wine that Hemingway had brought from Europe. The meal calmed the crew's nerves a bit, but the mood was still somber.

Suddenly, Hemingway rousted himself from where he was sitting on a cabin bench. "I'm feeling like a little music. Got your fiddle, Maestro?"

A skinny kid—younger than me, probably in his early

twenties—jumped immediately to his feet and ran into the galley, returning moments later with a violin case that seemed larger than its owner. There was something odd about the kid, but the instant he began to play, you didn't notice him at all. The bow danced over the strings and I felt the entire group relax. Hemingway had closed his eyes and didn't open them again until the playing stopped. Then he let out an enthusiastic whoop and gave the kid that winning smile.

"If you ever throw in writing, Mice, the fiddle's the gig for you. Great, ain't he?"

Everyone mumbled assent and there was scattered applause. The kid blushed and gave a nervous little bow.

"Mice showed up at my door awhile back and told me that he wanted to be a writer and I was just the one to teach him. Got to admire *cojones* like that, gentlemen. He's got the stuff too, if he wouldn't get so down on himself."

Seeming embarrassed at being discussed as if he wasn't there, the kid slipped back out of sight with his violin case.

"Tender soul," Hemingway said. "But a good sort." He stood up, stretched, and appeared revived by the wine, food, and music. "You dirty bastards up for the Dry Tortugas?"

The crew, feeding off his renewed energy, roared its approval. The course was set, the Chrysler engine engaged, and we were off.

Around dusk, we made it to the Marquesas Keys and set in to fish for smaller catches to eat. The take was easy and plentiful, and soon the smell of cooking fish had my mouth watering. We ate, drank rum, and then dove overboard to swim in the shallows. The activity and fabled restorative power of the salt water soon took its toll and everyone clambered back aboard for a good sleep.

I have never slept as well as I did on the hard deck of the *Pilar* that night, rocked into slumber by the gentle motion of the boat and soothed by the cool breezes. After what seemed like only minutes, I awoke to the smell of coffee and rolled to a sitting position. It took me a moment to remember where I was, and when I did, an indescribable sense of well-being washed over me. The crew was in fine spirits as we all breakfasted on smoked fish and avocados and then, after a short rest, we set out for the Tortugas.

At last, we docked at Fort Jefferson, a massive brick structure designed in 1846 and built until 1876, when the construction was halted. Without delay, the men began fishing in earnest. As the night before, it was a productive outing. One of the men, nicknamed Don Pico but whose real name was Waldo Peirce, dove underwater and came out with conch and crawfish that he pulled from the sea bed. I liked Peirce immediately. He had an infectious grin. His giant beard and absurd sponge hat lent an air of affability, offsetting his large frame, which might have otherwise been intimidating.

The day was spent swimming and fishing, capped off by a shooting exhibition by Hemingway, who took down several seagulls in mid-flight, aiming from all possible angles and never missing once.

As night fell, and another meal of cooked fish was being prepared, a small boat, a Cuban fisher, pulled up alongside. Hemingway invited the newcomers to join the meal, surprising them with more than passable Spanish. They came aboard and joined in both the meal and the drinking of rum. Then the Cuban captain brought out his own brand of alcohol, a cask of green Aguardiente. It was evil, powerful stuff—well over 100 proof—and as I swallowed the vile brew, I felt my fish dinner threaten to make a return visit.

That night, most of the men fell into a restless, drunken sleep and I was no exception. In the morning, no one felt much like fishing or swimming, and so we cast off for home.

Back in Key West, I discovered that Arenberg had been busily trying to determine my whereabouts. I found him at the courthouse, and when he saw me coming, I knew he was both happy to see me and furious at the same time.

"Where the hell have you been?"

"Fishing," I said. "Sorry, was I supposed to check in?"

He blustered for a moment, his frustration so that he was at a loss for words. Finally, he managed, "There's an active investigation going on! What kind of detective are you anyway? You're in the employ of the city now and I expect a bit more dedication to your position."

As he made his case, I began feeling a bit sheepish. It had, I realized, been extremely foolhardy and irresponsible to simply disappear out to sea under the circumstances, but I also felt I could not be held entirely responsible. I had essentially been kidnapped by Hemingway and his Mob. I had initially thought the outing to be a leisurely afternoon, with no idea it would turn into a booze-fueled romp to the Tortugas. It could be argued that I should have anticipated such a development, as Hemingway's reputation was well-founded, but I had been charmed by the man and his life-style. The situation had happened, nothing could change that, and what was more, I did not feel particularly repentant. It had been a hell of a good time. Not one I necessarily needed to repeat, but I was glad I had done it. In addition, the current experience was reminding me why I had disliked having an employer—they had expectations.

"Well," I said, trying with little success to sound contrite, "I'm back now."

Arenberg growled but seemed to decide to let the matter rest, at least for the time being. "I suppose there's nothing to be done for it now, so I might as well get you up to snuff on things."

"Something has happened?"

"You'd better believe it." He reached out and pulled me closer by my shirt front, as if preparing to impart some top-secret information. In a lowered voice, he said, "I have an eyewitness who saw Mike Danby out in a dinghy last night."

"So?"

"They also said he pushed something overboard. They heard the splash."

"And you think the splash was Mrs. Danby?"

"It figures. The guy is under suspicion for murdering his wife, so he takes the body and dumps it into the sea."

"What would be his motive? I don't think that would complicate any sort of *corpus delicti* requirements. She was seen dead by several witnesses who would testify. A little late to dispose of the evidence, isn't it?"

"To our minds, yes, but a cornered man does many a foolish thing in his hour of desperation."

"Have you searched the area where the dumping occurred?"

"Naturally."

"And?"

"The search party came up empty. Not that that's any big surprise; you know how these currents are."

Inwardly, I frowned. Now that Arenberg's preferred verdict—suicide—had been demonstrated to be highly unlikely, he was left with murder. The best way to deal with murder in Key West was to get it off the books as quickly as possible. Although Mike and I hadn't been pals for some time, I had no desire to see him railroaded.

"Doesn't smell right to me," I said, "but I'll head over to Mike's place and see what he has to say."

"You won't find him there," Arenberg said.

"Then where is he?"

"Jail."

"You had him arrested?" I was beginning to feel a little hot under the collar.

Arenberg took the defensive. "I've got a witness, Wolfe. And so far, all signs point to him. I like him for the murder, so, yes, I had him picked up."

"Signs? What signs?"

"I figure Danby found out his wife was sleeping around —for money, no less—and lost his head. Few men wouldn't. The fact that she was found murdered in a hotel room backs that up."

"How so?"

"Danby follows his wife one night to find out where she's headed, bursts into the room during the illicit encounter. He grabs the other guy's razor from the bathroom sink and attacks Mrs. Danby. It certainly wouldn't be the first time something like this has happened. You've spent time in the big city, so you must have heard similar stories."

I had to admit that Arenberg was correct on that score. My time in the East had opened my eyes to all manner of perversions, some much worse than the case confronting me now. Still, I didn't want to believe Mike would have done such a thing. Yet, it was important that I understand and accept the possibility that I was falling prey to my own bias.

"May I speak with Mike?"

"Of course," Arenberg said. "Head in to the jail and show them that card I gave you. They'll let you in."

I walked over to the jail and, upon presenting the card to the officer in charge, was led to Mike's cell. He sat on a cot, bent over with his head in his hands. The officer used a baton to rattle the bars.

"You got company, Danby. Up and at 'em."

Mike raised his head and his expression at seeing me sent a conflicted pang through my chest. This was not the look of a guilty man, but despite his obvious relief, I reminded myself to stay neutral.

"Sims, you came. Thank God. I thought maybe you'd

given me up for a guilty man."

"Sorry," I said. "I only now heard you were brought in. What's this I hear about you being in a boat last night?"

Mike glanced at the officer, who was still standing to the side of the cell door.

"Do you mind if we have a little privacy?" I said.

The officer scowled. "What are you, his lawyer?" Then, with a good degree of reluctance, he moved back to his desk and out of earshot.

"Speaking of a lawyer," I said, "did you happen to contact Louis Harris?"

"I didn't have time. They brought me in pretty quick."

"And they haven't allowed you to make contact since then?"

Mike shook his head. "That officer won't hardly give me a drink of water when I ask. They want me for this, Sims. I'm low-hanging fruit for them."

"It's beginning to look that way. I'll get in touch with Harris and see what he suggests for your case. In the meantime, you need to start talking and fast. Were you out last night in a boat?"

Mike dropped his gaze. "I guess I was at that."

"That was a stupid thing to do, Mike. What the hell were you doing?"

There was silence and then Mike said slowly, "I was going to end it. I'd gotten drunk and thought the easiest way out was to kill myself. So I got a little more drunk and then took a dinghy from the docks and rowed out until I was sure I wouldn't be able to swim back. Then I said some prayers, all that I could remember anyway, and went over the side."

"You know there's a witness who says they saw you. They say you dropped something over the side and that they heard a splash."

"The splash was me, Sims, honest it was. I didn't throw anything over except myself."

"That's not what Arenberg told me. He said that you pushed something overboard."

"Then he's lying. I didn't push nothing."

I thought back to my conversation of only minutes before, hearing Arenberg's words in my mind: "They also said he pushed something overboard. They heard the splash." They *said* he pushed something overboard. Not they *saw* him push something overboard. An important distinction. The way Arenberg had said it allowed for the possibility that an assumption had been drawn. Perhaps the witness only said they heard the splash and Arenberg simply made the assumption—albeit an entirely reasonable one—that the sound had been caused by an object being pushed over the side of the boat, rather than by someone jumping into the water.

"What happened?" I asked.

"What do you mean?"

"Well, you're still alive, so the suicide attempt was clearly a failure. What went wrong?"

"I changed my mind. The moment my head went underwater, I sobered up a little and realized I was being stupid, killing myself over Thelma. She clearly never cared about me or she wouldn't have done what she did. And if she didn't care, then what was I killing myself over? I kicked up with my legs and managed to grab the side of the boat. I just hung there awhile, just breathing, and then hauled myself back into the boat."

"You're lucky," I said. "Drunk, in the dark, alone. You're real lucky."

Mike nodded solemnly. "Don't I know it. I prayed all the way back to shore, thanking God for keeping me alive."

"Do you need anything in here?"

Mike look at me for a long moment. "A little justice, maybe. That's all."

"You got it, Mike," I said. "A little justice."

Since most of the day had been spent on the return boat trip, by the time I was done talking to Mike, the sun was already setting. I took Tiki out for a meal, and to say she was cool would be a gross understatement. I had to practically drag every word out of her. She considered my explanation that I'd been "kidnapped" by Hemingway and his Mob to be suspect at best, although I'm fairly certain I heard the word "idiotic" being muttered between bites of avocado toast and eggs. But at last, the mimosas began taking hold and she loosened up enough to let me know what had happened back at the hotel room after I'd left.

According to Tiki, Mike had recovered sufficiently by noon to stagger to his own place but was waylaid during the trip by Brucie, who had promptly flashed the front page of the *Citizen* in his face. Upon learning that news, Mike had locked himself in his room. Concerned for his safety, Brucie had stayed outside for most of the day, periodically pounding on the door and demanding to be let in. Near dusk, he'd given up and went home. As far as could be determined, no one had seen Mike until Arenberg had cornered him at Sloppy Joe's, already halfway drunk, and taken him to jail.

"Arenberg says there's a witness who saw Mike out in a boat last night," I said. "That leaves an entire day unaccounted for."

Tiki paused mid-bite. "You're not actually thinking Mike had anything to do with Thelma's murder, are you?"

"Honestly, I don't know what to think. There are plenty of questions to be answered, I'll say that. First of all, I'd like to know Mike's activities before I found him at the bar and brought him back to the hotel room. Second, I want to talk to Arenberg's witness and get the story straight from them. Mike admits to being out on a boat last night, but it's unclear whether they actually saw Mike toss something overboard or only heard a splash and made an assumption."

"What does Mike say?"

"He says he got drunk and went out to end it all."

"Then that's probably what he did. Most people don't go around advertising their suicide attempts just for the hell of it."

"Unless it's to cover up something worse."

Tiki's eyes had narrowed over the course of the conversation and were now mere slits of accusation. "With friends like you..."

I set down my fork with a good deal more force than

was necessary. "Why does everyone keep thinking Mike and I are the best of friends? We haven't palled around together since high school, for God's sake."

"But you were friends once. That should count for something."

"It does. I'm working the case, aren't I?"

"And suspecting your client."

"Just doing my job."

"I don't think Mike would have hired you if he thought he was going to get stabbed in the back."

I opened my mouth to say something, then closed it with a snap.

"What?" Tiki asked. "What were you going to say?"

"Nothing."

"The hell you were. Tell me."

"I'm not only working for Mike."

"Then who else?"

I remained silent.

"Not Arenberg."

Still, I kept quiet.

"Oh, Simon."

Those two words cut deeper than any of the other grief Tiki had been dishing out over the duration of the meal. I could handle Tiki's anger, but disgust and disappointment were different.

"I didn't make any promises to him," I added quickly. "Except that I'd look at both sides. I'd planned to do that anyway."

Tiki pushed abruptly back from the table. "I've lost my appetite. See you later, Simon." Then she stood up and walked out of the restaurant, leaving me looking like a damn fool.

Further playing the part of the fool, I refused to be shamed into leaving, instead remaining at the table and doggedly eating not only all of my food but what remained of Tiki's as well. When I'd finished, I paid the tab and left the restaurant.

The next morning, I headed to the law office of Louis Harris and found the attorney at his desk, halfway hidden behind a pile of paperwork. He smiled and stood up, motioning with one hand for me to sit down. Once I'd made myself comfortable, he resumed his seat.

"What can I do for you, Mr. Wolfe?"

"You know my name?"

"It's my business to know what's going on around here," Harris said. "I presume you are here to discuss the Danby case."

"That's right."

"A sticky situation to say the least."

"Are you familiar with all the details?"

"I know Mr. Danby is suspected of killing his wife, that the corpse has disappeared, and that Arenberg has arrested Mr. Danby on the rather suspect testimony of a witness he refuses to name."

"I'm impressed," I said. "Has Mr. Danby contacted you?"

"No."

"Then you've already discussed this with Arenberg."

"No."

"Then how the hell do you know these things?"

The little attorney leaned back in the big leather chair and leveled a smug grin directly at me. "Because I've spoken with someone else."

"Who?"

"Mrs. Danby."

I sat, stunned and speechless. The only explanation I could conjure was that Harris was a devotee of the occult and believed he'd contacted Thelma Danby's spirit. If that was the case, I wanted no part of it. I had half risen from the chair when Harris started chuckling.

"Oh, sit down, Mr. Wolfe. I'm not a spiritualist, not by practice, anyway."

I resumed my seat, although not without reluctance. "I'm afraid you're going to have to explain."

"Gladly. Although, you must agree to the strictest of confidences. This information is not to leave this room."

"Understood."

Harris steepled his fingers, as if channeling Sherlock Holmes, and paused in great dramatic fashion. "The woman who died was not Mrs. Danby."

I felt my mouth drop open but was powerless to close it. Finally, I managed to say, "But I saw the body. Both at the scene of the crime and at the morgue."

"You saw a body, but it wasn't Mrs. Danby. Not the real Mrs. Danby anyway."

"You're going to have to explain," I repeated.

Harris got up from his chair and began walking back and forth behind the desk. "The real Mrs. Danby currently lives in Tampa with her daughter in a house owned by her mother-in-law."

"Then who is the dead woman?"

"I'm getting to that," Harris said. "Mike Danby married his wife a few years ago, back when you were getting your education." He stopped paced abruptly and turned to me. "Which school was it, exactly?"

"Boston College." I was both impressed and troubled by Harris's breadth of knowledge of me.

The little man jerked his head once in a quick nod. "Ah, yes. I thought I'd heard that. Anyway, the couple lived in Tampa during the course of their short marriage, in the same house where Mrs. Danby—the real Mrs. Danby —lives now."

"How long were they married?"

"Not long. Maybe a year. After they separated, Mike returned to Key West and has been here ever since. To my knowledge, the two have not seen each other since. Mike hasn't seen his daughter since he left either. He won't travel to Tampa and Mrs. Danby—her name's Lara—won't send the daughter to Key West."

"And Mrs. Danby—Lara—still lives in her mother-in-law's house?"

"It's the Danby's house, actually. Mrs. Danby moved in after Mike moved out. Mike has been on the outs with his dear old momma since the separation. She completely sided with Lara, even offering to pay the legal fees if Lara wanted to file for divorce. But it never happened. I suppose nobody thought it was worth the hassle. Mike and Thelma took up together right after Mike moved back to Key West. In fact, it's generally thought that Thelma was the prime reason for the split."

"You say you've spoken with Lara Danby."

"That's correct."

"How does she know the details of the case?"

"She's been in contact with both Mike and Arenberg. And myself, naturally, which is how I know about the marriage situation."

"For what purpose?"

"For the purpose of defending Mike at trial, of course."

"Why would she want to do that?"

"I assume because, no matter her own feelings, she doesn't want the father of her child to be convicted of a murder. A thing like that could weigh heavy on a girl who's already going to be struggling as a result of a broken home and absent father who's been off playing the carefree bum and living in sin on an island paradise."

"Hemingway calls it the 'St. Tropez of the poor.'"

"Is that a compliment or an insult?"

"Knowing Hemingway, it's probably both."

Harris snorted. "Well, we like it anyway."

"What was your answer to Lara Danby? Are you going to defend Mike at trial?"

Harris walked to his chair and sat down as heavily as a man of his slight stature could manage. "I am, yes."

"Then it appears I came here for nothing."

"Not exactly."

"What do you mean?"

"You're an investigator of sorts, aren't you?"

I balked a little as the phrase "of sorts," but chose not to quibble. "Yes, I am."

"Then I may be in need of your services."

"That's very generous of you, Mr. Harris, but I should tell you that I'm already employed by Mr. Arenberg."

Harris frowned. "That is unfortunate. What are the terms of your employment?"

"I don't know what you mean."

"I mean, what is he paying you to do? Find out the truth or dig up dirt on the accused?"

"I think he wanted the latter, but I told him I'd only do the former."

"Fine, then there is no conflict. As your first task, I'd like you to visit Mrs. Danby in Tampa and find out anything she may know about the whole dirty business. Find out if she knows anyone in Key West who might be willing to, say, conduct a little overdue business here."

I was so surprised that I almost burst out laughing. "Are you saying you want me to find out if Mrs. Danby had Thelma killed?"

"Stranger things have happened."

"But I thought she was the one who was hiring you to clear her husband's name?"

"If she hired someone to kill the woman who, perhaps, ruined her marriage, that doesn't mean she wants her husband sent to Old Sparky. Besides, defending her husband would be good cover for her."

"But isn't this a little strange? I mean, a defense attorney hiring an investigator to look into a client?"

"You've a lot to learn about the legal profession, Mr. Wolfe, especially the defense. Knowledge is power. I wish to know everything there is to know and thereby avoid unpleasant surprises in court. Furthermore, one of the best ways to defend someone accused of a crime is to cast the blame elsewhere. A shadow of a doubt is all that is needed. If there is a plausible alternative, the jury is much more likely to acquit."

"And you would sacrifice one client for another?"

"Ah, but you see, we don't have to prove that Mrs. Danby did anything. We only have to make it plausible. As long as there is no real evidence, Mrs. Danby is in no danger."

"And if real evidence is unearthed?"

"Then I want to know about that prior to trial. That is where you come in, my dear Mr. Wolfe. Find out all you can, and report back to me."

"I hope you don't think I'm taking for granted your trust in me, Mr. Harris, but I'm going to have to think this over. It's getting so I can't tell my clients apart without a program."

"Then get one made up and start work. We don't have a lot of time. I have a feeling the prosecution is going to want to expedite this trial."

"Speaking of that, do you have any ideas concerning the identity of the mysterious witness who saw Mike out on a boat last night?"

"I do not have that information, although I will eventually, as Arenberg will be forced to turn it over. I just hope we receive it in time."

"Any thoughts as to why he'd want to conceal it?"

Harris shrugged. "Could be simply to keep us guessing. Or it could be that the witness is vulnerable or, perhaps, unreliable. It could be any number of things. That's something else you could investigate, while you're on the job."

"Looks like I have my work cut out for me."

"Then you'll do it?"

I hesitated, then nodded.

Harris jumped from his chair, reached across the desk, and grabbed my hand. "Good, good! Then let's get to work. Keep track of any expenses you may incur as a result of the investigation, as I will allocate an expense account for that purpose. That, along with whatever your daily rate is, should make it worth your while."

I LEFT Harris's office feeling more than a little conflicted. I had agreed to share all information with Arenberg. Well, technically, I had agreed to share any information gleaned from Mike. A reasonably convincing argument could be made that Lara Danby was a completely different matter, even if the information gathered from that source pertained to Mike. It was a simple enough matter to convince myself that was a fact, but the real sticking point was that I knew Arenberg wouldn't see it that way. Whether or not I was violating the letter of our agreement was one thing. I was certain Arenberg would believe I was violating the spirit of that agreement.

What spurred me to accept Harris's proposition, however, was the growing complexity of the case at hand.

As the pool of involved people grew, so did potential suspects, and playing my cards close to the chest was a strategy I felt would serve me well in the days to come, even if it meant skirting the limits of what would be generally considered a gentleman's agreement.

However, I soothed my conscience by reassuring myself that, were I to uncover evidence of Mike's guilt, I would turn that over to Arenberg. Other evidence that might appear damaging but not necessarily damning would be dealt with on a case by case basis. Yes, I had responsibilities to those who'd hired me, but I also had a responsibility to find out the truth, regardless of allegiance. And it would be impossible to do that were I to throw in with one camp without regard to the other.

My justifications thus worked out to the general satisfaction of my own sensibilities, I then made a bold decision that I wouldn't have dreamed of just a few days prior.

M rs. Hemingway welcomed me into the main house and sat me in the main room. Her husband, she explained, was still busy working in his writing studio but was expected back soon.

"He generally finishes work around one or two o'clock, which leaves him the afternoon for fishing," she said. "He loves that boat."

"The *Pilar*, you mean?"

She nodded, busily pouring me a drink I hadn't asked for. "Yes. He named it after me, you know."

"That must make you very proud. From what I can tell, the boat is his most prized possession."

She handed me the drink—scotch with a splash of soda. "It is, yes. I fear I would harbor jealousy against it, if it didn't bring him such obvious pleasure. Without the escape offered by the sea, I sometimes think he would go mad."

I took a sip of the drink, and it was then she seemed to

notice she hadn't asked my preference. She motioned to the glass in my hand.

"Oh, I'm sorry, Mr. Wolfe. I've become accustomed to almost all of Ernest's friends drinking. You needn't finish that."

"That's quite all right," I said. "It's very good scotch. How long have you two been together?"

"Ten years. Just a bit over ten years."

"A good run."

A shadow passed over her face and I tensed, wondering if perhaps I'd said the wrong thing. But she recovered quickly.

"Are you married, Mr. Wolfe?"

"No, ma'am—"

"Please, call me Pauline."

"Then you must call me Simon."

"Very well, Simon."

I sipped again at the scotch. It was, indeed, a good variety and, as is the case with most alcohol, became better as I drank it. "No, I'm not married. Never have been."

"However did you escape? A man with looks, charm, and intelligence doesn't generally survive long in the wild."

I laughed at the good-natured compliment and shrugged. "Perhaps it's my chequered past."

"That can be all the more attractive to the right woman," Pauline said. "It makes men interesting. And most men are dreadfully dull."

"That explains your attraction to Mr. Hemingway, I would assume."

"Ah, yes. Ernest is anything but dull. He's complicated, interesting, and also has what you referred to as a 'chequered past.' That certainly had its charms, but of course he's frightfully talented and brilliant."

"True enough. You met him in Paris?"

Pauline nodded. "Yes. He was married to someone else then—Hadley. Poor, sweet Hadley. I wronged her dreadfully."

I took another drink, feeling uncomfortable at Pauline's unexpected frankness. Then I said, quoting Charlotte Bronte, "Remorse is the poison of life."

Pauline smiled. "Repentance is said to be its cure, sir."

We both laughed quietly as we recited the passages from *Jane Eyre* and then Pauline poured herself a drink from the bottle of scotch.

"Heaven knows I've repented and, God being just, I may still pay the price for my betrayal. But Ernest was something I simply had to have. What is one to do, Mr. Wolfe, when forced to decide between being righteous or happy?"

"That's a question I wouldn't be able to answer without several more glasses of scotch," I said.

We heard the sound of a door opening at the rear of the house, following by the sound of a cabinet banging shut, and then the tinkle of ice. Hemingway was making a drink. Soon, his big form was filling the doorway to the room where we sat, our own drinks poised, our conversation arrested.

"Thin Man. Good to see you."

"Hey, Papa," I said—the scotch had given me sufficient

courage to, at last, try out the nickname he'd requested I use.

He grinned and moved farther into the room. He wore stained shorts and an untucked white shirt that hung open. He was barefoot, and I watched as he moved across the room, walking on the balls of his feet like a fighter on guard. I marveled at how quietly a man of his size could move. He sat down in a chair that put me on one side and Pauline on the other.

"How did work go today?"

"Went," Hemingway said, his tone making it clear that he had no desire to discuss it further.

Pauline immediately quieted, but it was less the thoughtful quiet of a loving spouse respecting the other's wishes and more the resentful silence of one not wishing to begin an argument. The strain between the two was unmistakable. I'd heard rumors of a lovely blonde having taken up with the Mob earlier that year—too early to have met her myself—and wondered if perhaps she had something to do with the tension that now blanketed the room like a second layer of humidity.

Hemingway stood abruptly. "I was just headed down to the docks, Thin Man. Want to join?"

Feeling as though I was being forced into making a choice between the two of them, I looked briefly at Pauline, but she refused to meet my gaze. Left with little choice, I rose slowly and, perhaps, a bit apologetically.

"Thank you for your hospitality, Mrs. Hemingway."

"You're most welcome, Mr. Wolfe."

It had escaped neither of us that formal names were once more appropriate.

"Come on, kid, will refresh your glass in kitchen. Cook is making peanut butter and onion sandwiches. Hope you like them."

We walked to the kitchen area, where a woman was just finishing the meal preparation. She stacked the sandwiches, individually wrapped in wax paper, and placed them into a canvas sack along with some avocados and two bottles of red wine. She handed the sack to Hemingway, who took it with a wide grin.

"Thank you, Miriam," he said.

"You're welcome, Mr. Ernest," the cook said. "You comin' back for supper?"

"With you cooking, it'd be a crime not to."

Miriam let out a loud laugh. "Such a kidder."

"I'm serious," Hemingway insisted, still smiling. "When have I ever kidded you?"

"When haven't you?" Miriam retorted.

We walked outside and on a low retaining wall that ran along a flower bed at the rear of the house. Hemingway opened the sack and took out two sandwiches, handing one to me and opening another for himself.

I wasn't sure what to expect from a peanut butter and onion sandwich, but it turned out to be fairly tasty. The onion was fresh and sweet and melded well with the creaminess of the peanut butter spread.

Hemingway munched happily, stopping halfway through his sandwich to uncork one of the bottles. He drank right from the bottle and handed it to me. I accepted

it and let the magical dryness of the cool red wine cleanse
my palate.

"Good, isn't it?"

"Very good."

"Love a good red wine." He took another bite of sandwich. "Suppose you could tell something was off. With me
and Pauline."

I shrugged. "I don't know how you two generally are
together, so—"

"Bit of a rough patch. You know how it is."

"I've never been married."

"But you know women. At least, you know about them."

"Sure."

"Then you know there's bound to be rough patches."

I nodded and could think of nothing else to say but
repeat, "Sure."

"She's not without just cause. Been making something
of an ass of myself, ever since Marty got hooked into
the group."

"Marty?"

"Martha Gellhorn. Female writer. Probably the best."

"Mrs. Hemingway is jealous of this Gellhorn woman?"

"Don't know if jealousy is right."

We sat for a few minutes in the shade, eating the sandwiches and drinking the wine. A peacock strutted in front
of us. Hemingway picked up several small rocks and pelted
the creature until it skittered away.

"Damn bird," he muttered. A moment later, "She's right,
you know."

"Who is?"

"Pauline. About Marty. Am head over heels for her."

I was considerably taken aback by this confession and wondered how I'd warranted such trust. Perhaps he simply needed someone to talk to, someone largely unaffected by the ripples any marital upheaval between the Hemingways might cause.

"Have you talked about this?"

"Talked? No. Fought, yes. An anger burns inside Pauline, but do not think it is an anger at me. At least, not mostly."

"Who, then?"

"Herself. Current situation not unlike the one in Paris, when fell in with Pauline while married to Hadley." A sudden veil of sadness fell across his face, and for a moment, I thought the large, burly man might burst into tears. "Ah, Hadley. Poor Tatie. Often wish I'd died before falling in love with anyone but her." He literally shook himself, as if casting away the encroaching shadows. "Pauline bears a good deal of guilt over the Hadley situation. She's Catholic, you know. If you want to buy stock in guilt, that's the place to go."

"What about you? Religious?"

"Became Catholic after marrying Pauline. We were having trouble in bed—couldn't get it up to save my life. Probably had something to do with own Hadley guilt. Tried everything. Went to a mystic, drank the blood from a calf's liver, all manner of things. One day, Pauline suggested that I go pray about it. I go to a nearby church and pray. Afterward, I went home to find Pauline in bed and waiting. I got off my clothes, climbed into bed, and we made love like the world was ending the next day. Never had trouble since. That's when I turned Catholic."

I couldn't help but chuckle at the story and Hemingway laughed along with me.

"Of course," he said, still smiling, "I've largely failed at the Catholic thing since, but was sincere to the core when I started."

By this time, I had almost forgotten why I'd come, but it came back to me in a flash and sobered me immediately. Hemingway noticed my shift in mood.

"You've something on your mind, Thin Man. What is it?"

"You're leaving for the mainland soon, aren't you?"

Hemingway nodded. "Tomorrow. Driving to Jacksonville. From there, Pauline and the kids are going to Mexico to watch the bullfights with Sidney Franklin, and I will fly to New York."

"And from there, Spain?"

Hemingway nodded again, and I saw the fire return to his eyes. "Back on the front lines, back in battle—"

Back with Martha Gellhorn, I thought.

"Why do you ask?" Hemingway said, interrupting himself as if he'd been about to inadvertently blurt out exactly what I'd been thinking.

"I've business in Tampa and was hoping to bum a ride."

The idea seemed to please Hemingway. He stood up and spread his arms wide, holding a sandwich in one hand and a bottle of wine in the other. "A wonderful proposition," he said. "You'll make excellent company. We'll drop you in Miami and you can fly from there. That's the way I'd take."

"Thank you," I said. "I don't have a car, see, and—"

"Don't worry, don't worry. I have a Buick Special that Toby got from Mulberg over on Caroline Street. You can ride with me and the others can follow with Franklin."

"I don't want to put anyone out."

"Don't worry about that either. At the rate things are going, it'll be better this way." Hemingway finished his bottle of wine and then picked up the sack of leftover lunch. "Now off to batten down the *Pilar*. Don't know exactly when will be back. Be ready at six in the a.m."

ON MY WAY to my next stop, I made a detour to the police station. I was hoping to avoid seeing Arenberg and, to my relief, he was nowhere in sight as I walked into the station and stopped at the desk.

The officer in charge looked up and I recognized him as the same one who'd let me into Mike's cell the day before.

"Here to see the murderer again?"

"No," I said, biting back the desire to remind the officer that prisoners are to be considered innocent until proven guilty. "I'd like to know if a report was filed when the witness made the accusations against him."

"You mean a statement?"

I nodded.

"Yeah, they made a statement. I'm the one who took it down."

"May I see it, please?"

The officer balked. "I don't know. You sure Mr. Arenberg's okay with this?"

Once more, I showed him the magic card.

There was a moment's hesitation and then the officer relented, no doubt more fearful of the consequences of disregarding Arenberg's card than the risk of sharing privileged information with an outsider. He moved to a file and thumbed through it, finally producing a single sheet covered with typed lines that ran at a slight angle across the page.

"Type this yourself?" I asked.

The officer nodded proudly. "Sure did. Self-taught typist."

"How...industrious of you."

I began to skim over the report, searching for the name of the witness who claimed to have seen Mike throw a body into the water. There, in poorly typed black and white, was the sentence, "Witness describes seeing Mike Danby push a woman's body over the side of a boat and into the water." It was clear that Arenberg had not been making assumptions and had only been repeating what the witness had reported. Unfortunately, nowhere in the report did it name or even describe the witness.

"Who reported the incident?" I asked, trying to sound casual.

The officer shook his head. "Sorry. He wanted to remain anonymous."

"So it was a man?"

"The *individual* wanted to remain anonymous," the officer amended.

"What's the big secret?"

"It's not that uncommon. Sometimes witnesses are concerned about reprisals or worry that having their names at all associated with a crime will tarnish their reputations."

13

I was waiting, travel bag in hand, in front of the Hemingway house at precisely six o'clock the following morning. From inside, I could hear loud voices and, although I couldn't make out words, it was clearly an argument. A minute later, the door banged over and Ernest appeared, looking hot, flushed, and furious. He had a duffle bag slung over his shoulder and wore wire-rimmed spectacles that hung askew on his face. He marched past me toward a gray convertible parked near the side of the house, waving me on as he walked. I jogged to catch up and then matched him stride for stride.

"Bitch took a swing and a scratch at me," he growled. "Missed, thank God. Don't need claw marks when I see Marty." He tossed the duffel into the back seat and climbed into the driver's. "Get in," he said. "Already loaded the rest."

I climbed into the passenger's seat, holding my travel bag on my lap.

Hemingway pointed at the bag. "That all you got?"

"I'll only be gone a couple of days," I said. "I'm not going to a war zone."

"You probably think you're in one now," Hemingway said wryly, starting the car and backing onto the street. "Sorry about the fireworks."

"Not my concern," I said.

"You're a good sort, Thin Man. Wish you were headed to Spain, but of course don't have clearance."

I almost laughed at the presumptuousness of the statement, as Hemingway clearly assumed I'd be able to drop everything and run off to Spain, if only I had the proper credentials. Then again, it probably wasn't so ridiculous of him to assume so, as most people would likely do exactly that. I wasn't so sure that I wouldn't succumb to the siren song of adventure with Ernest Hemingway, leaving Key West and missing corpses far in my wake.

We rode in style along State Road 4A, enjoying the wind in our hair and the stunning panorama of the blue-green water. Hemingway wasn't eager to talk, presumably a side effect of his spat with Pauline, and I didn't press. It was enough simply to be in the car; I didn't need to be entertained as well.

We stopped to fuel up in Key Largo. Hemingway had brought along another sack of sandwiches and wine, and we stood leaning against the side of the automobile while we ate and drank. Around us, as was the case all along the Keys, one could still see recovery efforts underway following the horrific hurricane two years earlier that had claimed over 400 lives and destroyed countless buildings.

"Great atmosph
should write abou
  I laughed. "N
that would be ?
  Hemingw
Key West. S'
  I almc
excited b
be in the
the title?"
  "Call it *To Have and* ?
represented. You'll like it. Just hor
  "I'm sure they will."
  "Never know what the critics will go for. .
care for *Green Hills*, damn them."

I made a scoffing sound and waved my hand as if
shooing away a bothersome gnat. "The critics don't know
what they like until it's so long after the fact as to not
matter."

Hemingway appraised me with a keen eye. "Good sense
from a writer not yet published."

I flushed a little, unsure if he was sincere or poking fun.
He noticed my ears reddening and added,

"Nothing wrong with that, kid. You'll get there. And
you're right about critics. Those bloodsuckers are men
who watch a battle from a high place then come down and
shoot the survivors."

Again, I almost choked on my sandwich, although this
time from a burst of laughter. Hemingway grinned, pleased
at my reaction to his witticism, and clapped me on the

CRAIG A

back to help me back to
breathing.
"Well, kid," he said
on a plane."

136

THE PLANE
aircraft b
close f
took
w

something resembling normal

. "Let's get to Miami and throw you

~

in question was a small, three-passenger
elonging to Chuck Madsen, a railroad tycoon and
riend of Pauline's wealthy uncle, Gus Pfeiffer. We
off and made the flight without incident, although we
re forced to land at Peter O. Knight Airport in the face
of an oncoming storm. After two aborted attempts, for
which the pilot blamed a treacherous crosswind, we
touched down, and I extracted my claws from the
upholstery.

Hemingway had also made arrangements for the same
pilot to see me back to Key West. I was flabbergasted by
this display of generosity, but Hemingway had merely
shrugged, saying, "It's on the old man's dime, and brother,
he can afford it."

After two miserable hours at the airport, waiting for a
ride the six miles into the city, I made it to my hotel and
checked in. I took off my shoes but fell into bed without
undressing further and slept the sleep of the redeemed.

14

The elder Mrs. Danby was a short, stout, and exceedingly Southern woman whose hospitality came very close to overcoming her displeasure at having to speak with me. The sweet iced tea and pecan pie she served on the wide front porch came very close to overcoming my discomfort at speaking with her.

We sat and progressed methodically through the required pleasantries. Mrs. Danby had a drawl not quite consistent with Florida natives, and I mentioned as much to her.

"Oh, I'm not a native Floridian," she said, her words as thick as the molasses in the pecan pie. "I come from Jonesboro, Arkansas. Moved down here to be close to my daughter-in-law once her marriage began taking on water, so to speak."

"Isn't it a bit unusual for a mother to side with the daughter-in-law—in these types of cases anyway?"

"Perhaps it is. But I am not your ordinary woman, Mr. Wolfe."

"How so?"

"I am from the South, Mr. Wolfe, but that doesn't mean I am backward. My son was of the old club of men who see themselves as exempt from societal rules. Namely, rules of propriety that only apply to women."

"I don't follow you."

"I don't suppose you would," Mrs. Danby said. "Ever since time began, men have played by a different set of rules. They want to go where they please, do whatever they like, and explore intimacy with anyone they choose. 'Boys will be boys,' Society says, with a wink and leer. But let a woman do the same and she is ruined. Her reputation, her prospects—gone forever. Slowly, over my life, I have seen that change, thanks to the heroic efforts of brave women. But still there remains a bias and double standard. My son, I am ashamed to say, is an adherent to the 'good old boys club.' He wishes to live as he pleases and yet claim the respectability that comes with having a wife, a child, and a home of his own. This goes against everything I believe in as a woman. And I cannot help but feel I let both him and society down—that I, an ardent feminist, could have raised such a misogynistic son—why, it pains me. Perhaps by facing this truth and following my conscience on this matter—at the expense of maternal instincts—I hope to atone for what I view as a moral failing."

Mrs. Danby paused in her speech, which had grown more passionate with each passing phrase, to take a drink from her iced tea.

I followed suit, enjoying the smooth, almost syrupy freshness as it ran across my dry tongue and trickled down my throat. The glass itself, filled to the brim with ice, dripped with condensation, and I held the cold side of the glass to my wrist in an effort to cool down the blood returning to my body's core. The temperature was on the rise and I yearned to remove my jacket. But somehow, I didn't feel free to do so in Mrs. Danby's presence; despite her stature, she presented an intimidating figure and silently demanded respect.

A car door slammed and we both looked to see a woman of around thirty-five standing on the sidewalk, just having exited a taxi. Her arms were full of shopping and her eyes were bright blue as she looked at me over the top of the packages. Then she started up the front walk toward the house.

I stood up quickly, almost knocking over the side table that held the remainder of the pecan pie, and hurried down the steps to help with the packages. The woman gratefully surrendered them.

"Thank you," she said. "Who knew clothes could be so heavy?"

She walked up to the porch and I followed close behind.

Mrs. Danby smiled thinly at the newcomer. "Lara, you're home early. And with quite a lot of packages, I see."

"I know, Mother Danby. Maas was clearing out their inventory for the fall line and I saw so many wonderful things."

"But the money, Lara."

"I know. But I didn't spend it all on myself. I found you

a wonderful cloche hat and matching shawl. I know how much you've always loved the cloche style."

"A sign of the times," Mrs. Danby said, her disapproval somewhat appeased. "Women wearing cloche are taken more seriously. It sends an independent message while still remaining feminine. Very well, my dear. Take the goods inside and then join us for some tea."

Lara went inside, and Mrs. Danby leaned toward me ever so slightly. "She spends too much but going to the shops is one of the few pleasures she has in life. And she does work hard, poor thing."

A few moments later, Lara reappeared on the porch. She had changed into a light cotton dress that nicely defined the curve of her breasts, and I had to purposefully look away. She helped herself to a glass of tea and then settled into a wicker chair that sat near Mrs. Danby and faced me.

Mrs. Danby motioned toward me. "Lara, dear, this is Mr. Simon Wolfe. Mr. Wolfe, this is my daughter-in-law, Lara Danby."

I half-rose and nodded my head. "Mrs. Danby, a pleasure."

"Oh, call me Lara," she said.

"Then you must call me Simon."

She smiled, showing off a row of white, even teeth. "Very well—Simon."

Mike, you damn fool, I thought. What were you think-ing? I'd leave Key West for a woman like this.

"Mr. Wolfe is a private investigator, dear," Mrs. Danby said, interrupting my thoughts—thoughts that were dangerously close to becoming lascivious. "He's here to discuss the murder of that Key West trollop."

I was shocked to hear Mrs. Danby, of fine Southern breeding, utter such a word about a dead woman, but it spoke volumes concerning her true feelings on the matter. I looked at Lara but saw no reaction. Either she agreed with the statement and thought it warranted, or she was used to hearing Mrs. Danby use the language, or perhaps both were true. The younger woman looked at me.

"What is your role in the case, Simon?"

"Ma'am?"

"Are you investigating for the defense or the prosecution?"

My mind whirred through the angles within the space of half a heartbeat. Saying I was representing both, while true, didn't seem to be a wise move in present company and might give the impression that I was not to be trusted, given my apparently fluid sense of loyalty. Saying I was working for the prosecution would almost certainly have the effect of sealing the mouths of both women, rendering my trip useless.

"For the defense," I said, suffering only a minor pang of conscience. It was, after all, the truth—just not the whole truth and nothing but the truth. Then again, I wasn't on the witness stand. "Mike and I played high school football together."

"Oh, so you're familiar with the situation," Lara said.

"Yes, I am."

"And more importantly, you're familiar with Key West and its...eccentricities."

"I believe I am. In the interest of full disclosure, I did spend time in the East for my education."

Mrs. Danby perked up at this. "Oh? At what institution?"

"Boston College."

"Ah. I have a nephew in Harvard."

"Impressive," I said, mentally grinding my teeth.

"But they're both good schools," Mrs. Danby added, with the air of one who believes they are being magnanimous. "You returned to Key West after your education? You did graduate, did you not?"

"Yes, I graduated," I lied. The mental grinding was threatening to turn physical. "And I didn't return to Key West right away. I spent some time working with the coroner's office and on various police cases."

"Is that what gave you a start in detective work?" Lara asked.

"I would say so. I became fascinated by the nature of crimes, the psychology of criminals, the patterns of human behavior that leads them to commit criminal acts."

"Sounds very exciting," Lara said.

"Sounds very dreadful to me," Mrs. Danby scoffed. "The very idea that it is a good use of time to study the minds of criminals—well, it's simply preposterous. We should all just accept that there is something wrong with their brains and lock them up."

"But, Mother Danby, if we could understand the criminal, we might be able to one day prevent many crimes from happening."

"Poppycock."

"And not only that," I ventured, "studying those who exhibit what we regard as aberrant behavior might just show us that we have more in common than we think."

"Now *that* sort of talk I will not abide in this house," Mrs. Danby said, her face a mask of disgust and anger. "Good people have nothing in common with bad people; they are two completely different breeds."

"Of course, Mother Danby," Lara said hurriedly. "You're right, naturally. I'm sure Simon didn't mean to say that we're all the same. Right, Simon?"

"I—"

The jangling of the telephone saved me from having to sell out my integrity even further. Lara rose to answer it, but Mrs. Danby hove from her seat and made for the door like a runaway locomotive.

"I'll get it, I'll get it," she said. "It's probably Mrs. Deavers from down the street with that fritters recipe she's been promising me for months."

Once the older woman was out of sight, Lara fixed me with blue eyes that were wrinkled at the edges with concern.

"How is Mike getting along?"

I shrugged. "I suppose as well as can be expected, all things considered."

"Yes," Lara said, her tone musing. "He's had quite a run of bad luck. Have they recovered the missing body yet?"

"You know about that?"

"Are you serious? The press can't get enough of it. You ought to hear some of the rumors and theories that are being bandied around."

"Like what?"

"Oh, surely you've heard them."

"I don't read the papers," I lied.

Lara thought for a moment. "Well, one columnist thinks there's a tiny colony of cannibals living on one of the keys and that they pay the mortuary for human flesh."

"Good Lord."

"Oh, and did you hear what Dorothy Parker wrote about the case?"

I shook my head. "I can't begin to imagine."

Lara cleared her throat, sat up straighter, and recited, "A body found / A body lost. / A paradise town, / But at what cost?"

I couldn't help but laugh. "She does have a way with words, doesn't she?"

"She certainly does." All at once, Lara sobered and fixed me with those blue eyes, eyes that all at once seemed much colder than before. "Why are you here, Mr. Wolfe? Really."

"I'm investigating a murder."

"What can you possibly hope to learn from us? We had nothing to do with the death of that woman. We never leave Tampa. In fact, we rarely leave this house."

I decided to repay Lara's sudden shift with one of my own. "Where's your daughter, Lara?"

"My—?"

"Daughter. You know, the one you have with Mike."

Lara looked down. "She's with her nanny."

"Is she often with the nanny?"

"Yes."

"When is she home?"

"Not until this evening."

Mrs. Danby came back onto the porch. She went to her rocker and sat down heavily. "It was old Mrs. Deavers, all right. She got halfway through the recipe and then forgot the last two steps. She said she'd call right back, but I told her to just wait and give it to me on Sunday at church. She'll never remember, of course, so we might as well forget about having those fritters."

"A shame," Lara said.

Mrs. Danby looked at the two of us, her eyes flitting back and forth. I could tell she'd noticed the change in atmosphere. "And how have things been going out here? You two getting along?"

"Just fine," I said. "I just had a couple more questions."

Mrs. Danby looked surprised. "Oh, really? I thought for sure this would be an all-day affair."

"No, ma'am. I don't want to take up any more of your time than I have to." I coughed lightly to reset the topic. "Have either of you traveled out of town lately?"

The two women looked at each other. At first, I thought they might be silently conferring, but they shook their heads simultaneously.

"No," Mrs. Danby said. "We haven't been out of town for months. Lara here is always complaining about it."

I directed my next question to Mrs. Danby. "Where is your grandchild today, Mrs. Danby?"

The older woman looked much less perturbed by the question than had Lara. "She's with the nanny."

"And I understand she spends much of her time there?"

Mrs. Danby's eyes narrowed. "I hardly think that's your business, Mr. Wolfe."

"Of course not, Mrs. Danby. Please accept my apologies." I turned back to Lara. "Your mother-in-law says you're a hard worker. Where are you employed?"

"A cigar factory in Ybor City."

"And fortunate to have it," Mrs. Danby cut in. "It's not an industry I support, but one can't be too particular about jobs these days.

"Tampa will survive," I said. "Key West did, when the cigar industry left to come here."

"Is that a hint of bitterness I hear in your voice, Mr. Wolfe?" Mrs. Danby said, smiling. "You needn't blame me. As I said before, I'm not from here; local politics interest me very little. On the national level, that's a different story. If we could just get rid of that man in the White House, we might be able to beat this Depression. Then Lara could get a job that neither supports such a nasty habit nor makes her hands cramp with rheumatism."

I stood up and made the required remarks. They, in turn, asked me to stay and then join them for the evening meal, which I refused. We all knew it was a mere social game, but that didn't excuse us from playing it. Lara went inside to ring for a taxi and one arrived within a few minutes. I extricated myself and got into the back of the car.

"Where to, Mister?" the cabby asked, his teeth clenched around a massive cigar that was at least sixty-five ring gauge and seven inches, not counting what he'd already smoked.

"Ybor City. The cigar factories."

The cabby nodded and stepped on the gas.

"That's quite a cigar," I said. "Where do you get them so big?"

"I know a guy," the cabby replied, his words mushy through his clenched teeth. "Makes 'em special."

"Must cost you a pretty penny."

"Saves in the long run. Cigar like this lasts me the whole morning."

I could see the logic, and it reminded me of Mark Twain's strategy of dealing with his doctor's order to cut back to one cigar a day; namely, buying larger and larger cigars until they attained the approximate dimensions of a crutch. If it worked for that great master of wit, I didn't see why a Florida cab driver couldn't do the same thing.

15

Had Ybor City's cigar industry been in the roaring state it had enjoyed in years prior to the economic down turn, I don't know that I would have ever located Lara Danby's place of employment. As it was, it took me the rest of the morning to convince enough floor managers to give me the time of day necessary to even ask the question. I hit pay dirt at a large, three-story brick building with large windows lining each floor and ornate masonry along the tops of the windows. It was clearly a place of industry, but some thought had gone into its construction and design, which was more than I could say for most of the factories I'd seen in the East.

I asked the driver to wait and then inquired at the front desk. A serious-looking woman with hair that was tightly pulled to a bun at the back of her head ushered me down a hallway that opened up onto the main floor. The room was massive. On either side of a center aisle were row upon row of cigar-rolling stations, and at each station sat an employee, heads bent over their work. On the right of the room, about halfway down, was constructed a wooden platform, atop of which stood a man holding a newspaper and reading aloud in a clear baritone voice.

"The entertainment?" I asked my guide, motioning to the reader.

"I beg your pardon?" she asked, then saw my indication. "Ah, the lector. Yes. We have readers every work day. They read from the newspapers and also novels and magazines. It makes the time pass more quickly, as cigar rolling can be a tedious task."

"I can imagine."

"If you'll just wait here, I'll ask Mr. Hardwick if he'll see you."

The woman bustled away to a small, shed-like structure built into the far wall, which I took to be the manager's office. She knocked and then entered.

While I waited, I look around at the workers. A few glanced up at me, but most kept their eyes dutifully on their work. Both men and women occupied the desks— and more than one child.

The door to the shed opened and the woman reappeared, followed closely by a short, corpulent man wearing a cream-colored suit and a black necktie. He brushed past the woman and crossed the massive factory floor, looking like a dreadnought that had just spotted a torpedo boat. As he lumbered toward me, his heavy brows knit into one solid mass of black that stretched over his close-set eyes, I considered aborting my mission but managed to hold my ground. Understandably, there was not a single worker with their eyes off their work while this fellow was on the floor.

The man was bellowing before he'd gotten within twenty paces of me. "Miss Grainger says you have a question about one of my employees?"

Not wanting to yell down the aisle, I held my tongue until he was nearer. At last, I said, "Yes. If it's not too much bother."

"Oh, it's a damn bother. A nuisance. I'm a busy man."

"Of course, it'll only take a minute."

"Then out with it! Out with it!"

I looked around. "Is there someplace we can speak privately?"

"Listen," Mr. Hardwick said, still shouting, "if it's a complaint about one of my workers, then it's best if everyone hears about it. I have no truck with nonsense and expect all my workers to uphold the highest standards of conduct."

"It's not a complaint."

"Then what? Come on, out with it!"

I tried to keep my voice just below normal speaking level, in hopes it would serve to moderate the conversation's decibel level. "I wanted to know if you employed a Mrs. Lara Danby."

"Who? Oh, Mrs. Danby! Yes, she works here. What's she done?"

"I didn't say she'd done anything."

"Then what you want with her?"

"Listen, Mr. Hardwick, I really think it would be better if—"

"Speak now or get the hell out, boy. I'm a busy man. My accounts need figuring and my dogs are barking up a storm."

"Then perhaps we should retire to your office. You know, for the sake of your dogs."

"Oh, very well. I can see you're not a man to be easily dissuaded. Let's head on back."

Mr. Hardwick made a wide right turn and headed back toward the shed, waving one arm as a signal for me to follow. We made it to the shed and Mr. Hardwick walked directly around a small desk and unceremoniously deposited himself in a cane back swivel chair. He moaned and propped one foot onto the desk.

"Shut the door and sit, if you've a mind," he said, leaning forward to remove a brown and white wingtip from the propped foot. "Lordy, but my dogs are howling today." He massaged the foot with fingers the size of sausages. He was still speaking loudly, and I realized what I'd taken for aggression was simply his own peculiar manner. "Now then," he said, once I'd taken a seat in the only other chair in the room, a singularly uncomfortable wooden folding chair with a single slat for a back that dug into my spine with the unnerving enthusiasm of a medieval torture device.

I leaned forward out of the range of the wooden slat. "As I said, it's about Lara Danby."

"A good worker. A natural roller. What do you want to know about her?"

"I was wondering if she had missed any workdays."

Mr. Hardwick shook his head immediately. "No, not

Lara. Always here and on time."

"I can wait if you need to check your records."

"Don't need to. I'd remember if one of my employees were to miss work."

"Are you sure? There must be at least a hundred people out there right now."

"It's my business to know my workers, Mr....what did you say your name was?"

"Wolfe. Simon Wolfe."

"Same first and last name, eh?"

I started to correct him, then realized he had merely been exhibiting what he must consider humor. I emitted a sympathetic chuckle. "And she hasn't taken a leave of absence for any reason? Family illness, perhaps?"

"No. Why, she sick?"

"Not that I know of."

"You're fishing for something, Mr. Wolfe Wolfe. But I really can't help you."

"What's her weekly schedule like?"

Mr. Hardwick squinted at me. "Say, what is this, anyway? You with the police?"

"Not exactly. I'm a private investigator."

The fat man's face lit up. "You don't say! Just like on the wireless, eh? I love those shows. Especially that Dick Tracy. You ever hear Dick Tracy?"

"Once or twice."

"That's a heck of a show. Has me on the edge of my seat four times a week. The wife, she likes that Crosby fellow, but I like a shoot 'em up with my dinner. It's the only way I can get down the wife's cooking." Mr. Hardwick laughed heartily at his own joke and I had to bite my tongue to keep from remarking on how successfully he was choking down Mrs. Hardwick's meals.

"Getting back to Lara Danby..."

"Right, right. What was the question?"

"Her weekly schedule."

"Oh, of course. She works three days: Monday, Wednesday, and Friday."

I nodded, thinking this over. A weekend was just long enough to make a trip to and from Key West, if desperate need arose.

I stood up. "Thanks for your time, Mr. Hardwick. I'll let you get back to those accounts now."

"You're welcome, detective. Sorry I couldn't give you any dirt on the old girl, but like I said, she's one of my best employees."

"That's okay. Thanks."

Mr. Hardwick made a half-hearted attempt to get out of his chair to see me out, but I waved him off. I had no desire to hear any more about his dogs.

I found the driver still waiting and asked him to take me to the courthouse. A quick check of public records confirmed the marriage of Mike and Lara Danby, with no divorce on file. That much checked out; one could never be too sure, after all. Then it was off to the police department to chase a hunch.

THE DESK SERGEANT greeted me with as much enthusiasm

as a hillbilly watching the approach of the county revenuer down the barrel of an old squirrel rifle.

"You want what, now?" the sergeant growled.

"Any police records you have that might reference Mike or Lara Danby."

"Who wants to know?"

"My name is Simon Wolfe. I'm a private investigator from Key West."

"Who're you investigating for?"

And then I decided to take a shot in the dark. "Big Louis sent me."

"Big—"

"Sorry," I said, laughing as if I'd embarrassed myself. "I mean Frank Arenberg. I'm so used to calling him Big Louis that sometimes I forgot not everyone knows him by that name."

The sergeant's face lit up. "So you know Big Louis, eh? Good man, Frank. Comes up here regular on business and grabs a beer with the boys."

"I'm sorry if I'm bothering you."

"No bother at all! If you're on official business, it's my job to help out."

"I can give you the number to the courthouse if you want to check out my credentials."

The sergeant waved his hand. "No need for that. I don't know a man alive who'd call Frank Arenberg 'Big Louis' if they didn't have leave to. Now, you wanted information about the Danbys?"

"Yes, sir. Anything you have."

The big policeman rose from behind his desk. "I'll be back. It'll just take a minute."

It was more than a minute but fewer than five when the sergeant returned with a file under his arm. He sat back down and pushed the file over to me. I opened it. Inside were several different police reports.

"You're welcome to read all that," the sergeant said, "or I'm happy to give you a summary."

I nodded. "I'd appreciate it."

"Well, I knew right where these files were, which was why I got back so quick. The reason I knew where they were is because we still talk about the Danbys here at the station."

"Oh?"

"Yeah. The Danbys were common talk around here, at least when the husband, Mike Danby, was still living in Tampa. We had an officer over there at least once a week for domestic disturbance."

"I suppose that would tend to make them memorable."

"Yeah, but that isn't why we remember them."

"Now you've got my curiosity up."

"Well, sir, it was a murder. At least, we think it was a murder. Still unsolved, to the department's everlasting shame."

"You can't win them all."

"No, but this one stings a little more than it might."

"How so?"

"The person we think did it is still living here in town."

"And that person?"

"Lara Danby."

The world stopped turning for a brief moment. "You're saying Lara Danby is suspected of committing murder here? In Tampa?"

"That's right. She was never brought to trial. Never even arrested. It happened back when she and Mike were still together. She found out Mike was stepping out on her and they had a big fight. It was so loud the neighbors called the station and we sent a man around to break it up, which he did. The next morning we get another call from a hotel manager, who says the cleaning lady has found the body of a woman."

"Let me guess," I said. "It was Mike Danby's lover."

The sergeant looked at me with new respect. "You're a quick study. And you're right. It was the very same."

"So what cast suspicion on Lara Danby?"

"Night clerk identified her."

"But she was never arrested?"

"No. Mike swore she was with him all night and only left her once to get a bottle of hooch from a nearby bar. Only gone fifteen minutes, which wasn't near enough time for his wife to commit murder and get back."

"I'm assuming Mike's story checked out?"

"Sure did. The bartender confirms that he bought the liquor and his boss gave a statement saying Mike had been at work all that day. Plus, the night clerk didn't see a man with the woman that he thought was Lara, so we were stuck. Without a way to impeach Mike's testimony and with him swearing Lara was with him all night, the county prosecutor saw no way forward based on a single eyewitness. Besides, there are plenty of pretty blonde women around. Clerk could have been wrong. No way would we have gotten a guilty verdict. So we had to let it drop."

"But you think she did it."

"I'd bet my pension on it."

While the sergeant had been talking, I'd been absent-mindedly looking through the files. Most of them were, as the sergeant had said, related to various domestic incidents. Then a name jumped out and hit me right between the eyes.

I closed the file and slid it back over the desk. "Well, thank you, Sergeant. I appreciate your time."

"Don't mention it. And tell Big Louis that I'm getting thirsty and it's time to swap some beers."

"Will do." I stood up. "Oh, one more thing. How was the woman murdered? The one in the hotel."

The sergeant picked up the file and placed it in his inbox. "Nasty business," he said. "She had her throat cut."

16

The question that beset me as the chartered plane thrummed its way to Key West was what exactly to do with the information I'd learned in Tampa. Who should I tell first? Arenberg? Harris? Or should I confront Mike and see if I could shock him into revealing something more? I couldn't help feeling a bit betrayed by Mike, since it seemed obvious that the Tampa murder could have bearing on this new killing—and Mike had not mentioned it. Perhaps he hadn't thought it relevant, but more likely, he knew that would mean that I'd learned a few other things about his past, things he'd rather keep quiet.

The plane landed late, and I got a taxi to my room. Although I hadn't been gone that long, I yearned to wash Tampa off my skin. A shower and a good night's sleep in my own bed would be just the thing. And I couldn't help but hope Tiki would be there waiting for me.

She wasn't, and a half hour later, I was showered and sleeping like a baby.

In the morning, I shaved, dressed, and headed back out to face the world. As I closed the door behind me, something sailed over my head and smacked the door frame with a loud *thwack!*

"Jimmy! Watch it! You just about took my head off with that throw."

"Sorry, Mr. Wolfe."

I stared at the boy, shocked by his appearance. His face looked drawn and his eyes were red-rimmed. "What's the matter, kid?"

"What do you mean?"

"You look like hell."

"Oh, that. I haven't been sleeping well the last couple of nights."

"No?"

"No."

"Someone causing you trouble?"

"No, it isn't that. I really don't want to talk about it."

"Jimmy, if someone's bothering you, all you need to do is tell me."

"Thanks, but—I have to finish up with these papers."

"Jimmy—"

"See you later, Mr. Wolfe."

I watched him go down the row of rooms and listened to the sound of papers hitting the doors as he went. The strange interaction gnawed at me; there was something wrong. For the moment, though, I had work to do, so I pushed down my concern for the kid and headed for the jail.

SURE ENOUGH, Mike was still there and had just finished his breakfast.

"How are they feeding you?" I asked.

"Like shit. In fact, it might actually be shit."

I glanced at the remains in the bowl. "I'm pretty sure it's grits."

"I don't know how the hell you mess up grits."

"Takes talent." I stood there, unsure how to proceed and checking to make sure the guard was out of earshot. Finally, I said, "You know, Mike. I don't have to help with this, you know. I don't owe you, you don't owe me; we're square, remember?"

Mike nodded slowly. "This where you tell me you're getting off the train? Letting me hang out to dry?"

"I ought to."

"I don't follow."

I looked him straight in the eye. "I went to Tampa, Mike."

His eyes dropped, and I knew that he understood what I was saying.

"Why didn't you tell me about the trouble in Tampa?"

It took him a minute, but at last he said, "I didn't think you'd take the job. And I needed your help."

"And Lara. Did she do it?"

"Sounds like you did your research."

"I know you swore she was with you the entire time. But now I'm asking you. Is that true?"

Mike nodded and raised his head to look at me. "Sims, I swear to you. It's true. The only time she was out of my sight was when I went to get the booze. And that was only a few minutes. No way she had time to…do it…and get back. Besides, she had no blood on her. I think that's even in the police report."

I looked at him steadily for several long moments, but his gaze never wavered. Finally, I nodded. "Okay. I guess I have no choice but to believe you, just as the Tampa police had no choice. As long as you know that if I find out you've lied to me on this—we're through."

I LEFT the jail feeling less than reassured. Mike appeared to be telling the truth, and his story exactly mirrored what he'd told the police back in Tampa. And yet there was a funny feeling in my stomach that wouldn't quite settle. Then I remembered what the desk sergeant had said about the night clerk at the hotel identifying Lara Danby and decided to try my own luck. If I got a positive identification, it would probably be in my best interest to cut Mike loose before I got in too much deeper.

With this in mind, I headed over to Mike's apartment. As expected, the door was locked, but a man in my profession is well-advised to be prepared for such things, and I retrieved two slim pieces of metal from my wallet. Setting to work on the lock, I had the door open within thirty seconds and stepped inside.

There was an eerie atmosphere within the apartment, although I attributed it mostly to tricks of my own imagination. The natural light was dim, so I flicked on the electric—it was bright outside, so there was no worry that someone might see the light from the street. And then I began searching the apartment. I started from the door and worked my way clockwise around the apartment. I checked every drawer and cabinet in the kitchen, even pulling out the silverware and dry goods to look underneath. I looked in the Maxwell House coffee tin that sat next to the stove, and I checked the sugar and flour jars. Nothing unusual. The bath was the same. The medicine cabinet contained the usual: aspirin, a Durham razor, a tube of Colgate's Rapid Shave Cream, two bottles of perfume. The closet contained towels, several bars of Ivory soap, and various feminine products. Then it was on to the bedroom. I started with the closet, going through every article of clothing, including pockets and inseams. Then I pulled down several boxes from the overhead shelf: hat boxes, shoe boxes, cigar boxes. Finally, at the bottom of an old cigar box containing random odds and ends, I found it —a picture of Lara standing between Mike and Mrs. Danby. I was lucky—it was a clear picture and, though monochromatic, I could almost see those blue eyes sparking. I tucked the picture into my pocket and had just set about straightening the mess I'd made of the closet when the handle jiggled on the front door and Brucie walked in. He looked around for a moment, then saw me standing in front of the bedroom closet looking guilty as sin. His eyes squinted.

"Simon. What are you doin' here?"

"Checking on a couple of things."

"What things?"

"You know, things related to the case."

"Things good for Mike?"

"I'm looking for the truth, Brucie. I hope that's good for Mike."

"Find anything?"

"No," I lied. "I struck out."

He stared at me. "I don't believe it. You look like a flyin' fish that's just been hooked. What'd you come up with?"

I realized he wasn't going to let this drop, so I pulled out the picture and held it up, close enough for him to see but far enough so that he couldn't snatch it away. Brucie took a look at the picture then turned his attention back to me.

"What're you thinkin' of doing with that?"

"Though I'd show it to the night clerk at the Overseas. See if he recognized Lara Danby from the night of Thelma's death."

"I can't let you have that, Simon."

"Why not?"

"It wouldn't look good."

"Look good for who?"

"Anyone in that picture. Bad for Mike, no matter what."

"Brucie, if someone in this picture killed Thelma, then we need to find out who it is, no matter if it was Mike or somebody else."

"It wasn't Mike."

"How do you know?"

"Because Mike wouldn't do that. He might get a little hot under the collar, but he wouldn't kill anyone in cold blood. Especially not a woman. Especially not Thelma. He was in a bad way about that woman. Would do anything for her."

"Some might say that's motive right there. Passion is a killer."

"Not for Mike," Brucie said firmly. "I know he didn't do it."

"I admire your loyalty, but I'd rather find out for myself."

I moved forward, but Brucie sidestepped, blocking my path to the door. I sighed. The little guy had some nerve, but I was running out of patience. I drew back my fist and clocked him on the side of the head. He went down like a sack of Bermuda onions, out cold.

THE NIGHT CLERK at the Overseas Hotel was a man named Horace Overshaw, himself a resident of the hotel. He was fiercely protective of his daytime slumber, as I discovered upon my third assault on his door with the flat of my palm. The door flew open and Overshaw stood in the doorway, towering over me by at least six inches. His height wasn't exactly intimidating, however, as he was so thin that he could have hidden successfully behind a fishing line. His shoulders were approximately the same width as his waist and he projected, all in all, the general demeanor of an emaciated corpse. His cheeks were hollow, and his eyes deeply set. His thin face was anchored by a hawkish nose and capped by a thin layer of jet black hair combed straight back.

A poor man's Basil Rathbone, I thought. Aloud, I said, "Mr. Overshaw?"

"What the hell do you want?" he demanded, his voice making it quite clear that he wished me death via some long and painful process.

"Sorry to bother you; I know you work nights and need your sleep."

"What do you *want?*"

"Right. I'm an investigator for Franklin Arenberg's office, investigating the death of Thelma Danby." I knew now that the woman's name had not legally been Danby but saw no reason to confuse the current tenuous situation.

Overshaw calmed a bit at hearing Arenberg's name. "Well, what of it? I've already been questioned."

"I only wanted to see if you could identify the woman in this picture." I removed the photograph from my pocket and handed it over.

Overshaw studied it for a moment and nodded slowly. "Yes. I recognize her. She was here that night."

"Did she check in?"

"Yes."

"And did you notice anything strange about her?"

"Nothing at all."

"Did she say anything unusual?"

"No. We conversed briefly as I checked her in, but it was all pleasantries."

"Can you recount the conversation?"

"It really isn't—"

"Humor me," I said, "and then you can get back to sleep."

Overshaw heaved a longsuffering sigh. "Very well. I

said, 'Are you checking in, Madam?' and she said, 'Yes, if you have a room.' I said, 'We do. How long will you be staying?' 'Just one night,' she said. She paid in advance, I gave her the key, and off she went."

"And that's it."

"Yes, that's—well, I do remember commenting on her accent. It was charming, very Old South. I guessed Alabama, but she told me Arkansas."

My heart skipped a beat and I grabbed the picture back. "You are talking about this woman, aren't you?" I said, tapping my finger on Lara Danby's face.

"That—good heavens, no. I've never seen that woman in my life. I'm talking about the other, older woman. She was the one I checked in that night."

17

I sat at the bar in Sloppy Joe's, drinking down a scotch and soda and feeling like an anvil had been dropped on my head. Mrs. Danby, that sweet old Southern lady, had been in Key West—and the same hotel—when Thelma had been murdered. I thought back on my trip to Tampa and my conversation with the desk sergeant. No one—myself included—had asked about Mrs. Danby's whereabouts during the approximate time of that murder. Perhaps both crimes had been committed by a mother out to protect her son. But if that was the case, then why choose Lara over Mike when it came to the separation? Maybe it wasn't Mike she'd been protecting. Maybe she'd been looking out for Lara. But why?

I had no idea how long I sat there, but all at once, I became aware of a tugging at my sleeve. I looked over to see Jimmy the paperboy standing next to me.

"Jimmy—you shouldn't be in here."

His face still looked haggard and his eyes were frightened, something I hadn't noticed before.

"Mr. Wolfe. There's...there's something I gotta tell somebody. And you're the only person I could think of who wouldn't think I was crazy."

I sat up and waved Big Al over.

"What can I get you?" the big man asked.

"Another of the same for me and a cola for the kid."

Big Al nodded and moved away to get our drinks.

"Sit down, Jimmy. Take it easy, now. You can tell me anything. Take it easy."

The kid sat down and drew in a deep breath. I could see his pulse throbbing in his neck. There was something wrong—bad wrong. I figured I'd known it this morning but had thought it none of my business and hadn't had the time. Now I felt bad. I should have pressed the kid harder.

Big Al brought our drinks and left us alone, as if sensing we wanted privacy—not much of a guess, given the look on the kid's face.

Jimmy took a long pull on his cola and then wiped his mouth with the back of his hand.

"Better?" I said.

He nodded.

"Then why don't you tell me what this is all about?"

"It's...it's going to sound crazy."

"I've heard a lot of crazy things."

"Not like this, I'd bet."

"Try me."

Jimmy drank his cola.

After a few moments, I reached out and put my hand

on his shoulder. "Jimmy. If you don't tell me what's happened, I can't help you. Are you in some kind of trouble?"

He shook his head. "No. At least, I don't think so."

"Then what?"

The kid drew in a deep breath and slowly let it out. At last, he said, "It was the evening before last. I'd gone around to all my customers that morning to collect the subscription money, but during dinner, I remembered I'd forgotten a house."

"Which house?"

"The one belonging to that German fellow. The one who works at the hospital. An odd duck."

"German fellow? You mean Carl Tanzler?"

"Tanzler, yeah." Jimmy's eyes widened. "What, you know him?"

"Not really. I've met him a couple of times."

"Would you say he's an odd duck?"

"He seemed a bit eccentric, yes."

"Well, I never like delivering there, much less asking for money. But the dough was due to the paper the next morning and I didn't dare be late. So I headed over to Tanzler's place to ask for the payment."

"Did he give you any trouble?"

"He never had the chance. I never talked to him."

"Why not?"

"By the time I got over to his place, the sun had set. The lights were on in his place, and through the window, I could see him dancing with someone."

"Dancing? Tanzler?"

"That was my reaction. I'd never heard of old Tanzler having a lady friend."

"Who was it?"

"I couldn't see from the street, because the curtains were drawn. I could just see them in a...what do you call it?"

"A silhouette?"

"Silhouette, yeah. Anyway, my curiosity got the better of me, so I sneaked up to the house to try and get a look at the dame who was crazy enough to spend the evening with Tanzler."

"And did you?"

Jimmy finished his cola and I could have sworn his pale face got even whiter. He nodded.

"Yeah. There was an opening between the curtains, and when I got close enough, I could see through into the house. Tanzler was dancing, all right."

"And the woman?"

Jimmy gulped. "I'm not sure it was a woman."

"A man?"

"No—not that. It was...it looked like...a corpse."

I steadied myself on the bar and finished my scotch and soda as calmly as I could. Then I slid off the bar stool.

"Thanks for telling me, Jimmy. You did the right thing."

"What are you going to do?"

"Don't worry about it. Just steer clear of Tanzler's place until you hear from me."

I put money on the bar for the drinks, leaving enough for Jimmy to have another cola, and then walked to the back corner, where a phone booth stood near the doors to the toilets. I rang the hospital and asked if Tanzler was working there that day. Yes, the woman on the line said, but he had just left for the day. Did I want to leave a message? I most certainly did not, so I thanked her and hung up. And then I took out of the bar like a cat with its tail on fire.

Out on the street, I turned up toward the hospital, hoping to spot Tanzler heading home. I saw him walking but soon realized he wasn't going home. Instead, he turned down Duval and began making his way toward the downtown shops. I toyed with the idea of heading straight to his house, but then realized I didn't know where he lived and, by the time I found out, he could very well be on his way back. I certainly didn't wish to be caught rummaging through someone else's residence for the second time in a single day. Instead, I cut around a block and came out behind the old man, spotting him again as he turned into a local drugstore. Taking shelter in a doorway, I waited for him to appear, which he dutifully did about ten minutes later.

I let him turn a corner and go out of sight before I detached myself from the shade of the doorway and made my way to the drugstore. I walked inside and waited not at all patiently while the druggist assisted an elderly lady in search of a certain kind of headache powder and then, once it had been discovered, explained in painful detail how to administer the dosage. At last, it was my turn. I stepped to the counter.

"Yes, sir," the druggist said, a light-skinned redhead who

had no business whatsoever being anywhere near the tropics, sub or otherwise. "How may I help you?"

"The name's Wolfe," I replied, hoping I sounded authoritative. "I noticed Carl Tanzler was in here a few moments ago."

"Why, yes, he was."

"May I ask what he purchased?"

"I'm sorry, sir, but this drugstore operates on the strictest of confidence. All my customers know their drugstore needs are well-protected."

"I'm working with Frank Arenberg," I said, praying I had one more solid ace up my sleeve.

"I'm sorry, but unless you have a warrant, I cannot reveal any confidential information."

"Do I need to call the courthouse?" I bluffed. "I'm guessing they'd take a dim view of a local business stonewalling their investigation."

"I repeat, sir, that a warrant is necessary."

I'd had enough. I reached over the counter and grabbed a large record book that lay open to the side of the cash drawer. A quick glance at the open page revealed the next to last purchase as being to a C. Tanzler and composed of five bottles of perfume and a box of molding plaster.

"Thanks," I said, shoving the log book back into its original position. "Thanks for nothing. Next time I get a cold, I'll just die."

~

FRANK ARENBERG LISTENED to my recounting of the

Tanzler tale with a face awash in skepticism. Before I could even tell him about my visit to the drugstore, he was shaking his head.

"You think old Carl took the body? What would be his motivation?"

"That's what I'd like to find out," I said. "And it would be a lot easier to gain entrance if I could take an officer along with me."

"Now listen, Wolfe. Carl's a strange old bird, but I don't think he'd do something like this. And he's certainly not a murderer."

"I never said he was the killer."

"But wouldn't that follow?"

"Maybe. Maybe not. That's what I want to determine."

Arenberg frowned and shoved his hands into his pants pockets. "I don't like it. If you're wrong, then the newspapers will have a field day." He stood deeply in thought for a full minute, then growled and said, "Fine. Take an officer with you. But no rough stuff. I want this as low profile as you can possibly make it."

THE OFFICER ASSIGNED WAS, naturally, Barnes. I expected to take a good deal of heat for getting him on this assignment, but either he had his own suspicions about Tanzler or Arenberg had given him strict instructions to follow my lead.

In the interest of keeping a low profile, we staked out Tanzler's house and waited until dark to make our move.

But before we could get out of the patrol car, the lights went on in the front room of the house and we heard a phonograph start up a lively waltz. And then I saw it—the silhouette like Jimmy had described. A thin figure—most likely Tanzler—and another form that appeared to be leaning heavily into him.

Barnes and I exited the car, closing the doors as quietly as we could and almost running across the street. We moved up to the house, creeping through the flora that lined the foundation until we could stand with our backs flat against the wall. I looked up and saw the slight crease where the edges of two curtains met at the base of the nearest window. I sidestepped closer, taking care to stay against the wall to avoid detection if Tanzler were to suddenly have a mind to look outside. Then I was there. I turned to face the wall and then raised onto the tips of my toes to peer through the crease.

And there it was, just as Jimmy had described. Tanzler moved gracefully to the music, his head tilted back and his face beaming upward at the ceiling. A wide smile crossed his face and his eyes were closed in rapture. In his arms, he held a woman. Or, at least, what used to be a woman. I couldn't see her face but knew from the position and posture that this woman was either unconscious…or dead. Then Tanzler turned to the music and I was suddenly face to face with his dancing partner. My heart stopped, fluttered, and then pounded in my chest like a runaway stallion. I recognized Thelma, even though it no longer looked much like her. The face was a ghastly white—the color of molding plaster, I thought sickly—and her face had been drawn on with what appeared to be various types of makeup, badly applied.

All at once feeling dizzy, I waved Barnes over and he took my place at the window. He took one look and then breathed a long string of epithets in the sincerest voice I'd ever heard. Then he unholstered his sidearm and made for the front door.

I stayed right behind him, my .38 appearing in my hand with notice. We charged onto the porch and Barnes took the flimsy wooden door with one charge. Through the kitchen and into the front room where we took up positions and leveled our weapons at Tanzler and his grisly companion.

Tanzler stood there, looked confused and befuddled. He wore a fedora and was dressed in a black tuxedo jacket and black pants, white shirt, black bowtie, and white tennis shoes without socks. He peered over his glasses at us, not angry or frightened but merely perplexed.

"Can I help you, gentlemen?"

For a moment, both Barnes and I stood there, our minds trying to make sense of the horrifying scene before us. At last, Barnes said,

"Mr. Tanzler?"

"Yes?"

"Who is that...woman you have there?"

Tanzler glanced down at the body he still clutched tightly to his chest. "Oh, this is my wife, Thelma."

"Your wife? Don't you mean Mike Danby's wife? His *dead* wife?"

"Oh, my, no. She may have been his wife once, but now

that she has died and then returned to life, she was free to marry another. And so she has."

"You…married…her?"

"But of course! I've loved her for some time. She was never happy with Mr. Danby, after all, and wanted the life only I could give her."

"Mr. Tanzler," I said, "won't you please put her down so we can talk more comfortably?"

He nodded curtly and moved over to a couch, where he laid the body down with the tenderness of a true lover. He arranged the hands across her middle and then patted them gently, whispering something like, "It will be all right, my darling." Then he straightened and turned to us. His face had taken on a resigned appearance and some of the life had seemed to go out of his eyes.

"I expect, gentlemen, that you will be asking me to come with you now."

"Yes," Barnes said. "Are you going to make us trouble?"

Tanzler shook his head. "No. No trouble. No trouble at all."

18

It was naturally assumed that Carl Tanzler, having been in possession of the body, was also the murderer. Arenberg went so far as to set Mike Danby free before several witnesses came forward and provided Tanzler with an unimpeachable alibi for the night of the murder. Apparently, he had been at Che Che's bar on Division Street late that night and had fallen asleep over the bar. Not wanting to disturb a paying customer, the bartender let him sleep until the bar closed and two big sailors had taken the count home and poured him into bed.

The news of the alibi about sent Arenberg over the moon.

"What the hell am I supposed to do now?" he roared at me. "Now I've got two crimes instead of one. You're supposed to be solving crimes, not discovering new ones!"

Dutifully, I left the courthouse and headed over to the Marine Hospital, where I requested to see any medical records pertaining to Thelma Danby. Knowing of my asso-

ciation with Arenberg, the records clerk gave me no
trouble and I thought once more that this extra piece of
persuasive clout might come in handy even after my official employment with the court ran its course.

I waited while he rifled through a massive grey filing
cabinet. It was hot and close inside the hospital, even with
overhead fans whirring softly, and I felt the prick of
perspiration under my collar. After a minute or two, the
clerk came up for air with a folder clutched in one hand.
He slid it over the desk.

"You can look at it here," he said, "but I can't let you
remove it from the building."

I nodded. "That's okay, I'll only need a minute."

The reading got real interesting real fast. There were
multiple instances of treatment for sexually transmitted
diseases—predictable, given her recently discovered occu-
pation—but the real interesting information was on the
next page where the report began to detail how Thelma
had begun receiving treatment for what was originally
considered asthma. Over time, she was discovered to have
tuberculosis and began receiving care for that illness. Some
of this care brought her into contact with Carl Tanzler,
who performed several X rays upon Thelma. Finally, near
the end of the file, I found a form that included emergency
contact details.

I looked up at the clerk. "Do you know a Miss Elsa
Raymond?"

"Miss Raymond, yes. She's a cousin to the patient in
question, Thelma Danby."

"May I borrow a pencil?"

The clerk handed one over, along with a pad of paper. I scribbled down the address, a small house not far from the Bight, and left the hospital.

Miss Raymond was not at home, but an elderly woman who identified herself as Thelma's Aunt Lucy let me in. We sat at a rickety, badly scratched kitchen table and drank cups of cool orange juice.

"I'm here to ask about Thelma's experiences at the Marine Hospital," I said. "I understand she was being treated for tuberculosis."

"Yes, poor dear," Aunt Lucy said. "She suffered terribly sometimes and then other times you'd never know anything was wrong with her."

"Do you know if Mike knew about her illness?"

"Oh, I don't think so. She was very private about it. Never wanted to talk about how she was feeling and didn't want anyone to know about the problem."

Makes sense, I thought. I'm guessing her client base would dry up quickly if they knew she was carrying around a contagious disease. Aloud, I said, "What about her time at the hospital? Did she make any friends there?"

Aunt Lucy hesitated, then said slowly, "I don't quite know what you mean by that."

"I mean friends. People she might have developed a relationship with beyond merely that of a patient with medical personnel."

More hesitation.

"Someone like Carl Tanzler, for example," I prompted.

"Then you know about that."

"Know about what?"

"About Thelma and Mr. Tanzler."

"What do *you* know about them?"

"Oh, they were a ridiculous pair. I don't think Thelma ever took it seriously, but Mr. Tanzler fell head over heels in love with her. He insisted on being the one to conduct all of her X rays and, I believe, even conducted more than necessary just to be with her more often."

"Did they ever meet outside of the hospital?"

"Mr. Tanzler always made sure to be at any social function Thelma was going to attend."

"How did he know where she'd be?"

Aunt Lucy shook her head. "I don't know. Perhaps they talked. I really don't know the extent of their relationship beyond the hospital walls, except to say Thelma thought it something of a joke. She was always a bit of a flirtatious creature, though, so she saw no harm in leading the old man on a bit. I'm sure she thought it as only harmless fun and that Mr. Tanzler knew deep down it was just a lark."

"I wouldn't be so sure about that," I said, relating the details of the previous night.

The old woman sat straight in the chair, wrinkled face aghast and right hand covering her wide-open mouth. "Poor Thelma," she said, once I'd finished my story. "That poor, poor girl. I never would have dreamed of such a horrible thing; Mr. Tanzler always seems like such a nice, reasonable man. A bit eccentric, perhaps, but—this!"

"It's a strange case, that's for sure," I said.

"And did he murder the poor dear?"

"It doesn't look that way. He has a pretty solid alibi."

"Then it's that husband of hers."

"Maybe. Maybe not." I stood up and gave a slight bow to my hostess. "Thank you for the juice, ma'am. I appreciate you speaking with me."

She stood up and walked me to the door, and I went out into the baking sunlight.

I headed back to my hotel room to splash a little cold water on my face, deciding to change my shirt while there. It was sticky and hot, and I yearned for a cool beer, but instead, I went over to Mike's apartment. I found him sitting on the landing, sharing a pack of cigarettes with Brucie. As I climbed the stairs, I considered the pair. The two men could not have been more different, and I wondered why they kept each other company. Mike was big and brash, while Brucie was small and meek. It was possible Brucie saw Mike as protection in what was often a rough and tumble existence in the Key West night scene, but I wondered what Mike got out of it.

"Good day, gents," I said, pulling up a couple of steps shy of the landing. I pulled out my own cigarettes and lit one up. "It's a hot one."

"Hotter inside," Mike said.

Brucie nodded. "Real hot."

I blew out a long puff of smoke and said as gently as possible, "How are you doing, Mike?"

"Never better," Mike growled.

"Sorry," I said. "That was a stupid question."

"He was just bein' polite, Mike," Brucie said. "You know Simon."

"I thought so," Mike said.

I raised an eyebrow. "What's eating you, Mike?"

He looked up at me and I saw his eyes were alight with anger. "I hear you're working for Arenberg."

"Where'd you hear that?"

"From the man himself. We got into a little...discussion about my case after that Tanzler fellow showed up with an alibi and he said it didn't speak highly of a man when his friends would take a job working to convict him."

"That's not really—?"

"That true, Simon?" Brucie said. "You really workin' for Arenberg?"

"I'm working for Louis Harris too," I said, angry at myself for feeling on the defensive. "I don't think you did it, Mike, and I thought working for Arenberg would give me the inside scoop on where the evidence was pointing."

"Where's it pointing? Any ideas?"

"A couple."

"Let's hear them."

I lit another cigarette with the cherry of the first. "I'm not ready to talk about that quite yet, Mike."

"Then you'll excuse me if I question your motives."

I sat down on the step where I'd been standing and propped my back against the railing. "You know, Mike, we've known each other for a long time, but I just realized I don't really know that much about you."

"Like what?"

"Like your background."

"Same as you. We played football together."

"I didn't know you prior to that first year of ball. And we lost contact when I left to go East. Were you at Key West?"

Mike hesitated.

"You might as well tell the truth, Mike," I said. "You know I've already spoken with your mother and Lara."

For a moment, Mike looked as if he might come at me and I braced for the charge. But then he settled back, and his eyes hardened, as if his mind were calculating. "Yeah, you told me you went to Tampa."

"Why'd you never get a divorce?"

"You don't think I tried? She wouldn't give me one."

"Did you know your mother was in Key West the night Thelma was killed?"

Mike's face went white, throwing his several days of beard into sharp relief.

"I'll take that as a no," I said. "She was identified by the night clerk of the Overseas Hotel." Then, casually, I turned to Brucie. "Say, what's your room number, Brucie?"

The little man visibly started. "What?"

"Your room at the Overseas. What's the number?"

"Oh, yeah. It's 102, I think."

"You think?"

"Yeah, it's 102. Why?"

"It's right across the hall from where Thelma was killed, isn't it? That's how you got there so fast, I suppose."

"Right, yeah. I...I heard screaming."

"As you said." I chained another cigarette. "Speaking of our early lives, where'd you grow up, Brucie?"

"Me?"

I said nothing but only stared at the little man.

"I...I grew up out West."

"Where?"

"California."

"You sure?"

"I think I should know where I grew up."

"You ever hear of an Arkansas toothpick, Brucie?"

"A what?"

"You heard me."

Brucie shrugged. "I suppose so. It's a knife, right?"

"Yes. A big knife. A sharp fighting knife, good for both thrusting and slashing."

"So?"

"So that's how you referred to the weapon that killed Thelma. You called it a toothpick."

Brucie shuffled around on the landing, as if preparing to bolt, but there was nowhere to run. Mike blocked one way and I blocked the other.

"That don't mean a thing," he said. "I must've just picked it up somewhere."

I nodded. "Maybe. Just thought I'd mention it. Although that doesn't explain why your name is on a police report in Tampa concerning the killing of a woman who'd been rumored to be involved with Mike. Or why it was your room that Mrs. Danby—Mike's mother—was asking for that night. One thing it does explain is why the witness who said they saw Mike dumping a body was so dead set on remaining anonymous. Couldn't very well have your name in those kinds of records, now could you? And you probably thought no one would think to check the Tampa records."

By now, Mike had gotten to his feet and his face, pale just a few moments before, was now black with suspicion and rage.

I continued. "Now that I've seen Lara Danby, I'm guessing you've been in love with her from the beginning. Whether or not she knew or reciprocated, I don't know. But Mike's mother knew, didn't she, Brucie? And you served as her sword to bring down justice on her wayward son. You killed the woman in Tampa and you killed Thelma, both at the behest of Mrs. Danby. The first was probably easy, wasn't it? I'd even believe Mrs. Danby had nothing to do with that one. Perhaps it was only a crime of passion. Maybe you were angry that Mike was hurting Lara, or maybe you thought Mike would take the blame and you could have Lara. But then the clerk identified Lara and the plan was off. Fortunately, Mike could swear he was with her the entire time, so all was well that ended well. But this time—this was a golden opportunity. And this time, Mrs. Danby planned it all out, didn't she? She probably figured out who'd killed the woman in Tampa and knew you'd be an easy mark. How did she reel you in, Brucie? Did she promise you Lara?"

Brucie darted forward, trying to slip past me. I took the charge with my left shoulder lowered and sent the smaller man rebounding back toward Mike, who reached out with one big, trembling hand, clutching for the scrawny throat. But before either Mike or I could act further, Brucie turned and vaulted the stair railing and dropped heavily onto the dirt alleyway below. He let out a deep *oof!* as he hit but was up in an instance and running like a jackrabbit.

Mike started down the stairs. "Let's get after him!"

I sat down to finish my cigarette. "In this heat? Forget it."

"But he'll get away."

"No, he won't. We're on an island, remember? I called Barnes at the station and told him to have a roadblock set up at the highway and other officers are heading to the docks. There's no place for him to run."

"What about Ma?"

"I also called Arenberg and asked him to make contact with the law enforcement in Tampa. They've probably already picked up both Lara and your mother."

"Lara's in on this?"

I shrugged. "That I don't know. In fact, there's quite a bit I don't know. You want to fill me in?"

19

Over the next couple of days, the Key West authorities, along with a few self-appointed vigilantes, conducted the most slow-motion manhunt I'd ever witnessed. Everyone knew Brucie had to be on the island somewhere, and no one seemed overly eager to find him, the search powered only by a grudging sense of duty.

At last, the fugitive was discovered, quite by accident, by two beachcombers as they wandered along a remote section of beachfront and stopped to overturn an old rowboat. By that time, Brucie was so desperate for food and water that he offered no resistance, and the two triumphant beachcombers brought him into town. They were promptly hailed as heroes and borne off to the nearest bar for celebratory drinks.

Information related to the case trickled in throughout the next few weeks. Lara and Mrs. Danby were picked up and questioned by the Tampa police but never went to trial. The only real case was against the elder Mrs. Danby and that dear lady took poison the evening after her questioning, no doubt expecting an imminent arrest. The house was left to Lara, with Mike not receiving as much as a mention in the will. Mike remains in Key West and Lara in Tampa, although I did learn that Mike was able to visit his daughter at long last.

Carl Tanzler is currently on trial for his part in the entire affair, with Louis Harris acting as his defense attorney. Not surprisingly, the nation has become enthralled by the case and, perhaps surprisingly, has more than a little sympathy for the crazy old man. Harris's case that makes Tanzler out to be a harmless old dotter who was overcome by the pureness of love has been remarkably successful, and the defendant may escape punishment for his macabre behavior.

For my part, I was happy to see the entire matter behind me. I received a letter from Hemingway the day before yesterday, detailing his exploits on the front. I suspect many of them are lies, but you can never tell. He claims he wants me on the next boat to Spain, and I admit the idea is tempting. Of course, I don't have a newspaper contract to cover the cost, so I suspect I'll be staying right where I am, on my island paradise of Key West.

AUTHOR'S NOTE

Night at Key West is based on true events. Many of the people, places, anecdotes, and situations have been taken from history, including newspaper accounts contemporary with the book's setting. Much care has been taken in the representation of Ernest Hemingway, who did indeed live in Key West during that time. The descriptions of his home are as accurate as I could make them, including events such as the fight night. Hemingway hosted many such bouts at his home, until his wife Pauline had a swimming pool put in where the ring had once been. Characters such as Al "Big" Skinner, Frank Arenberg, Louis Harris, Pena, Rhoda Barker, and Carl Tanzler were real individuals. Places like the Electric Kitchen, the Overseas Hotel, Sloppy Joe's, Pepe's, and others actually existed and are as faithfully described as I could make them. Wolfe's trip on Hemingway's boat, *Pilar*, is based on true events. Tanzler's macabre episode with a corpse is a matter of record.

Of course, as with any work of fiction, the facts are

used with a measure of creative license. For example, in the book, Hemingway and Wolfe drive the Overseas Highway from Key West to the mainland, even though the road wasn't entirely completed at that time, although it was well underway. Also, Hemingway and Dos Passos are shown to be experiencing the first real pangs of the rupture of their relationship; in truth, the two were already largely at odds by the time *Night at Key West* takes place.

However, with a few exceptions, I have done my best to create a realistic world as it existed in 1937 Key West, and I hope very much that you enjoyed taking this trip with me. I thank you for reading.

Craig A. Hart
Iowa City, 2018

ABOUT THE AUTHOR

Craig A. Hart is a writer, publisher, and stay-at-home dad to twin boys. He is the author of The Shelby Alexander Thriller Series, the SpyCo Thriller Series, and the new Simon Wolfe Mystery Series. He currently lives in Iowa City.

You can visit his website at: www.craigahart.com

ALSO BY CRAIG A. HART